There Will

Be Dancing

By Lyn Ellerbe

The Intercepted Heart

Love Beyond Repair

Chef Charming

There Will Be Dancing

There Will

Be Dancing

Lyn Ellerbe

Acknowledgements

Thanks to my husband, who indeed is my best friend, and who encourages me to keep writing! For my daughters, my friend Kathy and her family, once again, your support is prized. To my treasured friend Sandra, who welcomed a newcomer and became a life-long friend. Special thanks to my good friend, Carroll, who taught my children, and many others, to dance.

1

Whispering Through the Wedding

White and blue decorations had turned the sanctuary into an elegant winter wonderland. Silver lanterns flanked the altar and white lights sparkled from the evergreens along the walls. The decor created a stillness across the room as guests quietly found their seats. However, the atmosphere didn't have the same effect on all the attendees. A couple in one of the middle rows carried on a quiet, but humorous, commentary. The New Year's Day wedding was unusual and had given the pair plenty to discuss.

"If we get to set off fireworks instead of throwing rice, that would be fantastic!" The attractive brown-haired man whispered to the woman on his right.

"I think it's a little unfair for him to get such an easy anniversary date to remember, but just think what trouble he'll be in if he ever forgets!" The young woman's whispers reached the row behind them.

"Am I going to have to separate you two?" A voice hushed them from behind.

"No, mom," Aaron and Kim answered simultaneously. Aaron Mercer and Kimberly Calhoun were two thirds of a trio of high school best friends. Courtney Benton was the third. She and her husband, Geoff were seated behind Aaron, Kimberly, and their dates.

"Jinx." Kimberly tried to control the laughter bubbling up, knowing that she and Aaron were in danger of disrupting the wedding service. She heard Courtney's sigh from behind her. Kim thought how ironic it was for Courtney to be the mature voice now, given the antics she had instigated in high school.

Courtney just shook her head as she settled back into the pew. She was uncomfortable most of the time now, as she was approaching her last trimester of pregnancy. At least the winter wedding meant she didn't have to suffer from being too warm.

"Relax, dear." Her husband patted her hand.

"What were Gigi and Scott thinking, letting those two sit next to each other?" Courtney glanced at the handsome blond man sitting to the right of Kimberly.

Scott Delaney smiled over his shoulder and shrugged. Scott's date, Kimberly Calhoun was flanked on the other side by her best friend, Aaron Mercer. The two had been amusing each other with their comments on just about everything to do with the wedding decorations and program. Scott knew the two were close and he actually had Aaron Mercer to thank for his status as Kim's current boyfriend.

Sitting on Aaron's right, Kim's straight, soft black hair provided a striking contrast to the stunning red hair of the young lady on his left. Gigi Peterson, Aaron's latest conquest, seemed completely unaware of her date's antics. Courtney and Kim were not thrilled with Aaron's new girlfriend, but had vowed not to interfere. Kimberly didn't dislike Gigi. She just didn't think the young lady really understood Aaron.

As his closest friends, both Kimberly and Courtney were self-proclaimed Aaron Mercer experts. Of course, Aaron always listened intently to their advice and then chose to do what he liked. Over the years, though, he had learned to listen to their concerns, since it usually turned out they were right. Not that he would ever admit it.

The subtle change in music indicated the official ceremony was beginning. As the mother of the bride was seated, Kim reached behind Aaron and squeezed Courtney's outstretched hand, knowing her friend would be thinking of her own wedding day three years ago. Kim remembered Courtney's teary breakdown during the rehearsal, understandable given that her mom wasn't there for her big day. Courtney's mom had passed away suddenly when the three friends were freshmen in college. Aaron's mom, Gina, had stepped into Courtney's life as a surrogate mother, putting aside her sorrow over losing her best friend and cousin.

Courtney smiled her thanks. Her husband pulled her close and kissed the top of her light brown curls. As Kim turned back around, she saw the best man remind the groom to breathe as the bridesmaids made their way up the aisle.

"Greg looks like he's going to pass out." Kim elbowed Aaron.

"Understandable," Aaron said. "He's facing a life sentence."

"Be nice." Kim poked him in the ribs, and then scooted closer to her date. Scott slipped his arm around her as she leaned back against his warmth. "The wedding planner took the winter wonderland theme a little too seriously," Kim said. "I'm freezing."

Any further banter between Aaron and Kim was cut short as the music changed once more, letting them know the bride would be entering in moments. Kimberly realized that Gigi would have the treasured vantage point, being on the aisle, and when the guests stood for the bride's entrance Aaron would be completely blocking her own view.

"I wish we were sitting next to Courtney and Geoff," Kim complained to Scott. Courtney was several inches shorter than Kimberly. "I won't be able to see around Aaron."

"I'll put you on my shoulders if you like," Scott offered. The normally proper and serious lawyer's comment took Kimberly by surprise. Making such a spectacle of himself was more Aaron's style.

"No thanks." She grinned at the picture in her mind. "Your career would never recover from the press."

As the bridal march began and the congregation stood, Aaron held out his hand to Kimberly. He pulled her in front of him and settled one arm around her waist, his other across Gigi's shoulders. Kim smiled up at him.

"Thanks," she said. "You're my favorite." Aaron winked in response.

"Wow," Kimberly whispered to Gigi. "You did a marvelous job on the dress. It's gorgeous."

The aspiring fashion designer smiled her appreciation. Gigi had taken the bride's grandmother's dress, which was in quite poor condition after years of neglect and redesigned it. She was able to salvage much of the vintage lace and had even been able to match the color of the satin. The new dress had modern lines but held definite hints of the beloved legacy.

As the bride made her way to the altar, Kimberly stepped back around Aaron, patting him gently on the chest.

"Thanks, again." She stood on tiptoes and planted a kiss on his cheek.

"No problem," Aaron leaned over and answered in her ear. "I knew I wouldn't have heard the end of it if you couldn't see the dress...I mean the bride." She kicked him softly as they sat down. Scott quickly put his arm along the pew and pulled Kimberly closer as the service started.

Behind them, Geoff's arched eyebrow earned him an elbow from his wife.

"You know I'm right." Geoff leaned down and planted a kiss on his wife's cheek. "I'd even venture a bet on it."

"Whatever." Courtney rolled her eyes. "You don't know them like I do."

Aaron was Courtney's second cousin, and because their mothers were best friends as well as cousins, the two had grown up more like siblings. When Kim's family moved into the area during their eighth-grade year, the duo welcomed her into their circle. The three friends had been inseparable ever since.

When they were choosing colleges, most people assumed the three would head off together. Scholarship offers mandated Kim's choice and she ended up at a small school about an hour away from the large state university where both Courtney and Aaron enrolled. The three remained close through their college years, spending occasional weekends and all their long breaks together. When they all graduated almost four years ago, Courtney and Geoff were planning their wedding, and the trio realized that their close-knit circle was in for big changes.

Geoff Benton was very patient with the trio. When Aaron set him up with Courtney in college, he had been adopted into their crew, so he had a unique perspective on the main players. His lovely wife and Aaron were both a little on the reckless side. Growing up whatever hare-brained scheme one didn't think up, their families could be sure that the other one would. It was only when Kimberly showed up that some sanity was introduced into their mix.

Kimberly was naturally more serious and much less of a risk-taker. The cousins teased her about being the 'old lady' in their trio but learned quickly to let her caution rein in their enthusiasm. They had lost count of how many times her refusal to join in their schemes had saved them regret or embarrassment. Plus, Courtney and Aaron took pride in the idea that they had brought the cautious Kimberly out of her shell. All through middle and high school, the three were together more often than they were apart.

Recently Aaron had played matchmaker again and introduced Kim to Scott, a college friend that had moved to Atlanta after completing his law degree. Geoff and Courtney were surprised that the relationship lasted more than a few weeks. Not only did Kim tend to stay away from any long-term commitment, but she and Scott were too much alike, too.

As the ceremony ended, the group made their way to the reception hall. Aaron and Kim each grabbed one of Courtney's hands. As the three walked in front of their partners, Aaron offered a partial apology.

"It was her fault." He pointed at Kim. "You know I would never, ever disrupt such a solemn occasion."

"Nice try, big guy." Kimberly made a face at him over Courtney's curly locks. "I'm still her favorite."

"Try to get your date to behave, Scott," Aaron said to his friend who laughed and pulled Kimberly back to his side.

"Impossible," Scott replied.

"C'mon, people," Aaron called to Geoff and Gigi who had fallen behind. "There's going to be dancing."

"And food, I hope," Courtney said as Aaron led the group into the dining hall.

2

They're Playing Our Song

At the reception, Geoff watched Courtney twirling through the moves of a country line dance with her friends, smiling at the trios' obvious attachment. He knew that his wife missed her friends, especially now as the baby's arrival was so close.

Kim and Aaron had loved Geoff from the beginning, and he was now an integral part of their fellowship. The only problem they had with the young software developer was that his job meant Courtney was now a couple hours away from her best friends.

"Now you guys are stuck with each other again," Courtney had teased during their recent monthly get together. "I got out as soon as I got the chance."

"Funny," Kimberly had said. "Not only do I have to endure his presence at church, but I have to work with him everyday." Her business degree meant she was the perfect choice for the new Atlanta branch of the Mercer's family business, a chemical supply company researching and promoting eco-friendly alternatives. When Aaron's dad realized the need for a distribution office closer to the big city, he entrusted this new branch of Mercer-Chem to Aaron.

Working at the plant since he was a teenager, Aaron had been groomed to eventually take over the business. He had never gone through the typical 'I hate my family and want nothing to do with the family business' stage. His father never gave him any preferential treatment and Aaron had to work his way up through the ranks. From his first job in the maintenance department, he spent a summer with the shipping crew, and then college breaks working in the plant and the lab. He was very prepared to move into management as he graduated with his degree in Chemistry. The management experience he had earned in the years since graduation meant he was ready, capable, and eager to take on the operation of the city office. Kimberly was his second hire. His first was Scott's Aunt Joyce, as his administrative assistant.

As the active line dance ended, Scott and Geoff were settling themselves at the table, both with plates piled high with food. Geoff lured his wife back to the table with a selection of her favorite goodies.

"Have a seat, dear," he said, "or baby Abigail may arrive doing the jitterbug."

"Okay," she agreed, "but only if you promise to dance at least once with your very fat wife."

"You are not fat." He tweaked her nose. "And yes, I'll dance any slow dance you want, *after* you eat something."

The deejay had just introduced the next set, and the first notes of a classic love song began. Kimberly and Aaron had headed to the punch bowl after the line dance and as the song began, he pulled her back onto the floor.

"They're playing our song." He swung her into the familiar moves of a waltz. The two of them, along with Courtney, had learned to waltz as teenagers. Their home church had a musical theater outreach that involved the entire congregation, young and old. The program had become so popular among the youth group that the teacher planned numbers for the show every year specifically for the teens.

Kim laughed as she recognized the song used as the waltz from one of the productions.

"Are you sure Miss Georgiana won't mind? I'm monopolizing your time." Kim asked, using Gigi's proper name for emphasis. She glanced around and saw the pretty redhead laughing with her friends on the balcony.

"No more than Scott minds," Aaron said. "In fact, I think Scott should mind a lot more than he does."

"Don't be silly," Kim said. "You know Scott and I are not ready for a serious relationship. Give the guy a break."

"Nope," Aaron said. "Can't do it. You deserve to have someone fall madly in love with you and then be insanely jealous whenever anyone else dares to look at you."

"You are ridiculous."

"I'm going to test my friend Mr. Delaney." He leaned in and whispered in her ear, knowing the action would look much more intimate than it was. "Let's see if he's paying attention." Aaron slid his hand from the proper position between Kimberly's shoulder blades, down to her waist.

"Stop it, Aaron." Kim frowned as his hand moved slightly lower.

"Well, well," Aaron said. "We have made contact." Along with Courtney and Geoff, Scott had indeed been watching the couple.

"He wants me to react, doesn't he?" Scott asked.

"Yes." Courtney said. "He'll be mad if you don't. He introduced you two, so he feels he has a right to make sure you still deserve her. For all his goofiness, he's very protective of her."

Scott took a long drink of his soda and watched the pair over the rim of the glass. A few moments latter, he heeded Courtney's advice.

"Here comes Prince Charming." Aaron grinned at Kimberly. "Right on cue."

"Happy now?" Kim asked as her date approached them, weaving through the couples on the dance floor.

"Immensely." Aaron gave her a quick kiss on the cheek. "Love you."

"Love you too, dork," she said as Aaron bowed and

handed her over to Scott.

"Did I pass?" Scott asked Kim as they danced.

"Was he that obvious? I'm so sorry," she said. "He's such a goofball."

"No problem." Scott tugged her closer. "You two throw around that 'Love you' statement quite freely, you know."

"You're not jealous, are you?" Kim laughed. "All three of us say that all the time. That and 'you're my favorite,' too. It's a family thing, I guess."

"Got it," Scott said. They finished their dance in silence.

Kim enjoyed spending time with Scott but didn't see their relationship going beyond friendship. She knew it was unfair to monopolize his time, especially since he was an extremely eligible bachelor. She hoped they would remain friends, but knew she needed to release him from their relationship, no matter how casual it was. *I need to start praying about this,* Kim thought.

"You're deep in thought." Scott pulled her into a hug as their waltz ended. She just smiled and nodded, not ready for the needed conversation yet.

Courtney and Aaron were watching them intently.

"Oh, no," Courtney said. "She has that look."

"I think you're overreacting." Aaron watched Scott and Kimberly wait for the next song to start. "This is different. It's already lasted longer than normal. Hasn't it been almost three months?"

"Be nice," Courtney said, as Geoff returned with a

refill of punch for her.

"You have to admit, though, she doesn't have the best luck with men." Aaron stole Courtney's last cheese covered cracker, knowing Geoff would be returning to the refreshment table to get another plateful of goodies. "There have been so many."

"True." Courtney sighed. Pregnancy had made her even more sentimental than usual. Having found Geoff and having him love her so unconditionally made her want that gift for her friend.

"Derek, Steve, Rodney, and Lamar." Aaron counted off men on his fingers. "And that was just high school."

"Ah, Lamar." Courtney laughed. "They were such a cute couple." Kim had dated the center of their high school basketball team during their senior year, but only for a couple weeks. His mom, with her Jamaican heritage, and his dad's Hawaiian culture, meant their tropical restaurant was a favorite in the area. Kim's parents frequented the diner and the families were close.

Lamar towered over Kim by eighteen inches and outweighed her by a hundred and ten pounds. Their relationship sparked some controversy among the less open-minded in the school. Kim's experience as an "Army brat" meant she was unprepared for the response to their relationship. On military bases, skin color tended to blend in behind the uniforms.

"Remember how shocked she was to find out that the comments were not about their difference in height? Her naiveté is so refreshing sometimes, especially since she is so brainy."

"Scary smart," Aaron said, "yet adoringly innocent."

"True." Courtney pushed her half-empty plate toward Geoff's seat. "Sometimes I think her innocence is a defense mechanism, though. It protects her from seeing the worst in people, but also keeps her from being disappointed. I don't even think she's aware of it."

"I can see that." Aaron drained his cup of punch.

"Lamar and Kim are still close, you know. She was in his wedding a couple years ago."

"No, I didn't know that." Aaron frowned. "Why didn't she tell me that?"

"If it bothers you so much, you should ask her."

"No way," Aaron said. "She'd either accuse me of being nosy or berate me for not caring enough to know about it in the first place."

"I think there are quite a few things that she kept from you, me, or both of us over the last few years. Thankfully she didn't start up a serious relationship in college," Courtney said. "I was always concerned that since we weren't there to protect her, she would fall in love with some unsavory character."

"She knew better," Aaron said. "I'd take whatever action I thought necessary if she did, and we know how she hates the attention. Imagine her reaction if she had to bail me out of jail and sit by my side through a criminal trial." Courtney's laugh reached Kim's ears. The pair at the table waved to the couple on the dance floor.

"Solving the world's problems?" Geoff returned with

the food, interrupting the discussion, which he could tell was on the serious side.

"No, just Kim's," Aaron said, around a mouthful of a spicy eggroll. "We were listing all the guys she's dated. I ran out of fingers."

"You're terrible!" Courtney wiped the sauce from Aaron's cheek, and then nodded toward the patio. "Besides, you have no room to criticize. Here comes Gigi. I think you need to pay attention to your own relationship and leave Kim to me."

"No way." Aaron stood, ready to hand Gigi into her chair. "I'm in this until the end."

"In what?" Miss Georgiana asked.

"Nothing," Courtney and Aaron answered together. The redhead looked from one to the other and shrugged.

"Sometimes I just don't get you people," she said with an elegant pout.

3

The Breakup

Scott and Kim managed to squeeze in at least one evening together each week, but his law firm specialized in business and tax law, so this was their busiest time of the year. A couple weeks after the wedding, they made plans for dinner and a movie.

They opted for the earlier matinee, hoping to beat the crowds. This was the opening weekend for the latest release in the current rash of superhero movies.

"Looks like we'll need to get popcorn tonight," Scott said as Kim's stomach growled on the way to the theater.

"Sorry about that." Kim laughed. "I forgot to eat lunch. We are up to our ears in files, getting ready for our first audit."

They enjoyed the movie, and the popcorn. Both were avid fans of the genre, and both had strong opinions about their favorite heroes and villains. It made for a lively dinner.

"You know I'm right." Kim waved a nacho chip at Scott. They were sitting in a darkened corner of their favorite Mexican restaurant. "He was the perfect choice for that role."

"Are you sure you're not being influenced by the brawny good looks and blue eyes?" Scott snatched the chip from her fingers.

"His or yours?" Kim laughed as Scott raised an eyebrow.

"Mine, naturally." The waitress interrupted their banter when she brought their entrees. The couple settled into the authentic Mexican dishes, sharing bites off Kim's sampler plate.

"So, back to our debate," Scott said. "Are you saying that your love of the movie was not influenced in any way by the looks of the actor portraying your favorite super hero?"

"Should I be offended that you would think I'm that shallow, Mr. Delaney." Kim reached across the table and stole a bite from Scott's platter of fajitas. "Looks may turn my head, but character will keep it turned."

"Good point." Scott's silence following his comment drew her notice.

"And? You obviously have something else to say on the matter." When he still didn't answer, Kim sighed. "Go ahead, Scott. I'm sure what you're going to say is not going to surprise me."

His response did surprise her.

"Where do you see yourself in five years, Kim?"

"What do you mean?"

"We've been dating almost three months, and we've never discussed our life's goals or ambitions. What things are important to you for the future?"

"You're scaring me, Scott," Kim said with a shaky laugh. "Is everything ok? Is there something going on at work? They're not dumb enough to fire you, are they?"

"Your confidence is not very encouraging, missy." Scott pushed his nearly empty plate to the side and reached for Kim's hand. "Be honest with me, Kim. What are you hoping for from life?"

"Life, liberty, the pursuit of happiness?" Kim's attempt at humor didn't fool Scott. He squeezed her hand gently.

"Answer the question." He held her hand as she tried to pull away. "Marriage? Children? Career? Fame?"

"Yes?" Her voice was shaky and she fought back tears. "We're really going to do this now, aren't we?"

"Yes, Kim." Scott's voice was quiet and serious. "I care about you too much for us to continue to pretend this is going to work."

***

They spent the next hour talking on a deeper level than they ever had throughout the weeks they had been dating. Although they both held family as a high priority, at this point in life, Scott was focused on his career. As a young attorney at a prominent law firm, he would have to dedicate most of his time to his work in order to establish a reputation. He was striving to balance his faith with his occupation, but had found that one of the partners at the firm was also an elder in his church. All this was news to Kim and she realized they had not shared some of the most important aspects of their lives.

Through his confession, Kim came to her own realizations. Scott's vulnerability was so inviting that she opened up and admitted her own misgivings. Having moved every two to three years, since her father was a career military man, Kim resisted forming deep relationships.

"Aaron and Courtney seem to be a major exception to this rule, though," Scott pointed out.

"True. My jumping from one relationship to another is something they tease me about," she said. "I know I've been unwilling to commit to a relationship. I'm sorry if that means I led you on in any way."

Scott refused to let her blame herself, reminding her of the many fun times they had shared, and reasserting that he wasn't ready for a serious relationship now anyway. Scott knew Kim felt the same way he did and gently moved her to the point where she accepted his assertion. They left the restaurant no longer a couple, yet ironically closer than ever.

"Shall we be cliché and say that we'll remain friends?" Kim asked when Scott walked her to her apartment door.

"We may not be a couple anymore, but I am counting on you being my friend. One of my closest, as a matter of fact." Scott turned her toward him after she opened the door. He kissed her gently.

"I'm going to miss that." She sighed. "If you need a reference for a future girlfriend, I will let her know you are an excellent kisser."

Although their kisses were chaste by anyone's standards, Kim enjoyed the brief touches, and knowing that someone found her attractive enough to kiss.

"Well, if you ever really, really need a kiss, just let me know." He laughed and kissed her once more before she finally closed the door.

4

Don't Be Too Hard on Him

"What's she doing here so early?" Aaron asked as he stopped at his assistant's desk. Joyce handed him the day's files and he headed towards Kimberly's cubicle.

Kimberly's countenance this morning was enough to let Joyce know what had happened, even without the heads up she got from Scott's early morning call. Still, she was glad she knew the details of the ending of their relationship before having to face Kimberly. And Aaron.

"Are you okay, sweetie?" The older woman had asked Kim when she arrived uncharacteristically early this morning. Kim was never late. An unapologetic creature of habit, she walked through the door at the same time each morning. Many in the office joked that they could set their clocks to "Kim time" since it was so accurate.

"So, he told you, did he?" Kim's lack of sleep caused her to sound more upset than she was. "I'm fine, Joyce, really. Don't be too hard on him, okay?"

Kim stood staring out across the rainy parking lot. Although their decision was an answer to prayer, she was still sad. Her ego was a little sore, too, since Scott had been the one to suggest they break up. Kimberly had been through a lot of relationships, normally ending them after a few weeks. She was very good at breaking up and remained friends with most of the young men afterwards. Surely God had the right man in her future, but for now, she was losing hope. *Why can't I ever just fall in love with one of these great guys God brings into my life? Am I just being too picky? Scott was the ideal man. Good-looking, kind, has a steady job, loves God.*

"And not a bad kisser, either." Kim smiled to herself.

"Who's not a bad kisser?" Aaron asked from the doorway. "Why are you here so early?"

"Nothing, why?" Kim turned from the window and smiled. Aaron wouldn't be happy about her news, so she needed to take her time thinking of exactly how to tell him.

"What's wrong?" Aaron knew her too well. It was obvious that something had happened. His intense gaze made her squirm. She turned back to the window.

"Scott." His first guess was correct. "He's an idiot." Aaron pulled out his phone and dialed Scott's number.

"No!" Kimberly grabbed the phone and ended the call before it connected. "I broke up with him."

"Liar," Aaron said. "Give me my phone. I have a thing or two I need to say to our noble lawyer friend."

"Really, Aaron. Let it go." Already tired from lack of sleep, she didn't want to fight a battle this morning. "I'm fine. We both know that Scott and I are too much alike for this to have worked out."

Aaron leaned on the edge of the low filing cabinet by her door, arms folded. His silent stare demanded an explanation.

"Honest," Kim repeated. "I am fine. Promise. I don't want to talk about it right now. Please."

"Fine," Aaron conceded, "but we will talk about this later. Understand?" Kim nodded. The desk phone rang before he could continue.

"Go away." Kim shooed him out of her office.

A supplier issue occupied most of the afternoon. Kim was able to put off thinking about her relationship, or lack of one, by dealing with irate customers whose orders would be delayed. It was a welcome reprieve.

As the workday ended Aaron was trapped when his dad called from the main office. Kim took the chance to sneak out. Her phone rang as she walked into her apartment.

"Nice try," Aaron said. "I'm on my way. Order pizza."

"No, Aaron. I'm fine. Leave me alone, please." Kim's words were unusually short-tempered. "Really. Fine."

"Kim, talk to me."

"Not this time, Aaron. See you on Sunday." She flopped on her couch, kicked off her shoes, and prepared for an evening of mindless entertainment. As she caught up on her favorite shows, she was relieved but a little surprised that he didn't show up at her door anyway.

5

Raised Him from a Pup

By Sunday morning, Kimberly's attitude had recovered. Aaron's parents were visiting, and Kim slid into the pew next to Larry Mercer. He had spent Friday afternoon at the office, checking on details and meeting with the staff. Next month's inventory and audit would be important in the decision on whether or not the city branch was a good idea. Aaron's mom had immediately sensed something was bothering Kim and had uncovered the news of Scott and Kim's relationship.

"Are you okay, sweetie?" Gina Mercer had asked. "You seem a little sad." Kim admitted that she was more frustrated than sad.

"I'm wondering if I will ever find someone, but I realized that I need to stop feeling sorry for myself." Kim had confessed. Today as she settled into the pew, Gina reached across her husband and squeezed Kim's hand.

"Quit hogging the pew," Aaron said when he arrived a few minutes later and playfully scooted Kim over. He noticed the satchel. "You're teaching today?"

Kim nodded. The children met during the service for their own teaching time and she was one of the teachers for the three-year old class. The last time she taught, which was six weeks ago, Scott was her assistant, albeit a slightly reluctant one. Dealing with anyone younger than twenty-five made the staid lawyer nervous. Today she faced handling a classroom full of three-year-olds without help.

Thinking she might ask one of the teenagers to help out, Kim was delighted to see two middle-school girls standing at the classroom door as the children were dismissed.

"Can we help you, Miss Kim?" The two young ladies had noticed Kim had made several trips between the supply room and kitchen before the service started.

"Oh, that would be delightful!" Kim thanked the teens as she bent down to greet her little students who were hurrying into the classroom.

"No need, ladies." Aaron's voice sounded behind her. "I'm here to save the day."

Disappointment battled with wide-eyed infatuation in

the faces of the young ladies. Aaron's wavy brown hair and dark blue eyes never failed to get a response.

"Thank you, Aaron," Kim said.

She turned to the teens. "He'll be fine, ladies. I trained him from a pup. He's basically a three-year old himself, so he'll fit right in."

The young girls giggled as they rejoined the youth sitting in the first few pews of the sanctuary. The church had a strong youth group, whose members were regular workers in the nursery and children's ministries.

"Are you sure your parents don't mind?" Kim asked as they settled the children into a circle for story time.

"Are you kidding? I would've never heard the end of it if I hadn't ridden to your rescue. I'm at your command, milady." He swept a deep bow, making the young kids laugh at his antics.

Today's scripture story was David and Goliath, always a favorite. Having Aaron, whose nearly six-foot form dwarfed the youngsters, act the part of the Philistine made the lesson time noisy and fun. Kim couldn't help but think how the kids would have reacted to Scott, who topped Aaron by several inches.

"I'm going to take these two to the restroom," Kim said quietly to Aaron as the class was finishing their craft. She didn't want to make a class-wide announcement, as it usually meant they would all suddenly need to go.

When she and the two girls returned, Aaron was reading the story to the class once again. Kim paused at the doorway.

A boy whose family was new to the church, was snuggled on Aaron's lap. The boy had been unsure about the whole situation at the beginning of class, and it had taken awhile to get him to join the activities. Aaron's charm had worked. Kim's heart skipped a beat.

6

Cheap Chopsticks

After church, the Mercers stood quietly to the side as the parents collected their children. Kim saw them grin as several students excitedly explained Aaron's antics.

"Mr. Aaron was Goliath! He's so tall, but Jimmy knocked him down with just one stone!" Kim had to explain the "stone" was only a paper wad.

"Aaron is going to go pick up Gigi. They'll meet us at the restaurant." Gina Mercer was helping Kim clean up the room so they could get to their favorite Chinese buffet before the Sunday rush. "Gigi got a donation in late last night and had to unpack it this morning." Aaron's girlfriend managed a small second-hand boutique downtown. It featured only upscale, expensive pieces. Kim had visited once, but even the discounted prices were too much for her modest wallet.

Kim had settled into her meal when Gigi and Aaron arrived. The bubbly redhead let Aaron slip off her coat, and then she hugged Mrs. Mercer warmly. Kim waved at Gigi with her chopsticks from across the table.

"Oh, Kim, I'm so sorry!" Gigi reached around the centerpiece and patted Kim's hand. "Aaron told me about you and Scott. What a meanie!" The delicate wooden sticks broke with a loud pop.

"I've got the perfect guy for you, though." Gigi didn't even pause. "Harold Farley is available and I think you two would be so cute together!"

"Absolutely not!" Aaron growled. "Let's get our food, Gigi. We can leave the matchmaking until later."

Kim struggled to recover. Aaron's dad handed her another set of chopsticks. "Cheaply made, obviously." She smiled at him in thanks.

When the pair returned, Gigi had obviously not understood Aaron's warning tone. She returned immediately to the topic.

"I don't understand Aaron's objections, Harold is so handsome, and his family is very well-off," she said, her tone slightly patronizing.

Aaron watched Kim intently, but she refused to meet his stare. Kim let Gigi ramble on.

"That's so nice of you, Gigi," Kim said. Aaron recognized the falsely sweet tone. If he hadn't been so frustrated with his girlfriend, he would have warned her. Instead, he simply picked at his food with his chopsticks.

"I can introduce you if you like." Gigi sounded confident in her matchmaking skills.

Finally, Aaron intervened again.

"Harold Farley is a playboy and unworthy of any decent young lady." His comment earned him a nod from his dad.

"Actually, I've decided to swear off any serious relationship for awhile." Kim saw Aaron's hand stop halfway to his mouth. Ready for the conversation to turn to other issues, Kim decided to launch a salvo.

Take this, Mr. "I tell my girlfriend everything," Kim thought.

"I'm planning on playing the field." She smiled at Gigi. "Maybe many fields. You know what they say about so many fish in the sea. I'm going take up fishing."

Aaron's chopsticks snapped. He glared at Kim. She blinked innocently in return. Mr. Mercer was unable to squelch his laugh. "Ha! Cheap chopsticks strike again."

"Let's change the subject," Gina said.

"Great idea, Mother," Aaron replied. Only Gigi was oblivious to the tension at the table for the rest of the meal.

An hour later, Aaron's message popped up on Kim's phone. *Answer your phone!* It was identical to the previous three she had ignored. This time she typed an answer.

Leave me alone. I'm going to turn off my phone now. Aaron tossed his phone onto his kitchen table and hung his head. Gigi had returned to work after lunch and

Aaron had headed home with his parents.

"She'll forgive you eventually, son," his dad said. "Give her time." The Mercers were gathering their things as they prepared to return home. "We can stay an extra day if you need us to."

"No, I'll face the dragon myself." Aaron sighed. "I don't know what I was thinking telling Gigi about Scott and Kim."

"Whatever you do, don't call her a dragon."

"Thanks. It's good to know you guys have my back." Aaron held the car door for his mom.

"Oh, no, son, you have it all wrong." Gina patted his cheek. "We're on her side."

7

The Lessons

On Monday morning, a tentative knock broke through the soft sounds of music in Kim's office. She was filing the latest invoices, her back to the open door.

"Go away, Aaron." Kim didn't bother to turn around.

"I know you're mad, and I deserve your wrath. Let me apologize, please."

"Apologize all you want, but then go away."

"You have to forgive me." Aaron took a step into the office, not wanting the rest of the office to hear their discussion.

"Says who?" Kim twirled her chair around and picked up another stack of files, never meeting his eyes.

"C'mon, Kim. You know I'm an idiot, but I didn't have any idea Gigi would make such a big deal of it."

His plea was met with silence.

"I know that you'll eventually forgive me." He

stepped back out of her office. "Admit it. You can't resist my charm."

"Watch me," Kim said, over her shoulder. "This may have been the biggest mistake you've made. I'm so mad at you that I cannot even imagine forgiving you right now. I think you've made it very clear that Gigi is now your confidante. You two are welcome to each other. I'm done."

"That's a load of nonsense and you know it." When Kim glanced back again, Aaron was gone.

The chill between the two friends lasted several days. Thankfully, everyone was busy trying to get their normal tasks completed ahead of schedule in preparation for next month's expected frenzy. Three days later, Aaron found Kim staring at a brochure, as she ended a phone call.

"What's that?" He plopped down in the chair across from her desk. When she didn't immediately order him out of her office, he knew she had finally forgiven him.

"I just tried to cancel the dance lessons Scott scheduled for us." She held up the brochure. "At the wedding, he gallantly pretended he had always wanted to learn some fancier moves and offered to take a few classes with me. The classes start this week and it's too late to get any of his money back."

"Serves him right. He shouldn't have broken up with you." Aaron was making a long chain of her paperclips—a habit that drove her crazy. She reached across and yanked them out of his hands. He grabbed them back and started undoing them. "So, take the classes anyway. When are they exactly?"

"They're flexible." Kim looked for the explanation in the pamphlet. "Scott paid for eight lessons. I think he said we could do hour-long classes, or longer ones, and could choose different dances to learn, too."

"Let's do it." Aaron finished unhooking the clips and dropped them back into their container. "It'll be fun!"

"Let's do it?" Kim stared at him in surprise. "You want to take lessons? What will Gigi say?"

"She'll be thrilled," Aaron said. "The lessons will make me shine even more at all her high society functions." The Petersons were members of the upper echelons of the big city society and Aaron had complained on many occasions about having to suffer through the elegant parties.

"You mean those agonizing events with caviar on fancy china, champagne in crystal goblets? Poor baby."

"They're torture," Aaron said. "You should feel sorry for me."

"Sorry," Kim said. "Yes, that's the word I would use."

"Ouch." Aaron flipped through the pages of the dance class pamphlet then stood and pulled Kim to her feet. He twirled her through a couple waltz moves. "We should do this. I bet they'll put us right into the intermediate class. We'll be the next Fred Astaire and Ginger Rogers."

"You really think Gigi will let you take lessons with me?" Kim pulled herself away from Aaron's attempt to spin her once more.

"*Let* me?" Aaron asked. "Despite my titanic mistake

on Sunday, you've got the wrong idea about me and Gigi." Kim arched one eyebrow.

"I want to do this and I do not need her permission. Besides, it will have the added bonus of making Mr. Scott Delaney infinitely jealous as he realizes what he's missing!" Aaron captured her again, and dipped her dramatically over his arm. Kim laughed.

"I doubt that will ever happen, but I'm game if you're sure." Kim moved back behind her desk and pulled out her calendar. "The lessons are supposed to start tomorrow night. Is that good for you?"

"Absolutely." Aaron was glad to see a smile on her face as he left her office. It was worth the sacrifice of a few evenings' peace and quiet.

***

As the two swirled around the dance floor the following evening, they grinned at the reaction of the teacher. The very proper French instructor had put on a classical waltz and asked the couples to show him what they knew of ballroom dancing.

Aaron and Kimberly had been partners for the church performances all three years and had mastered the waltz. In college, the pair, along with Courtney, had attended as many dances as they could. Having events on two campuses to choose from meant they had kept up their skill level.

"You!" Jacques Castille, the wiry European dance master pointed at Aaron and Kim. "Go down the hall.

You are not beginners!" They were dismissed summarily. Elinor Maltby, Jacques' assistant, was a kind, older woman, and a former ballroom dance competitor. She smiled as she led them to the Intermediate class.

"Jacques will be down here in a moment," she explained. "He's the Intermediate class instructor, but likes to look over the newcomers at the beginning of each session. He's not as brusque as he sounds. You will enjoy him."

There were four other couples in the studio and introductions were made. Kim was afraid they would be the least experienced of the class but found that these concerns were ungrounded.

Mrs. Maltby's assessment was true. The first class turned out to be a blast. Aaron and Kim had not laughed so much in a long time. Jacques was impressed with all the students. He promised they would polish up their waltz skills at the next lesson, and then move on to Latin dances.

"I can't wait until Thursday!" Aaron said as he dropped Kimberly of at her apartment. "I honestly didn't expect to have such a good time."

"So glad you were able to endure the torment of spending the evening with me!" Kim responded.

"You know what I mean," Aaron said. "I'll see you in the morning. If I'm not too sore to move!" He heard her laughing at him as she closed and locked her door.

What fun. Kim thought later that evening as she sipped a cup of hot chocolate while watching the late news. She decided to send a message to Scott before it got too late. Since she wasn't upset about their break up, she resisted the urge to gloat over how much fun the lessons had been.

I wasn't able to get a refund for the dance lessons. I'm sorry. Aaron decided he wanted to take the classes with me. I hope that's all right. We had our first lessons tonight. It was fun. Thanks again.

Several miles away, Scott read the incoming message. A raised eyebrow and slight smile accompanied his reply.

No problem. Don't worry about the refund. I'm glad you guys had a good time.

8

Let It Snow

"No, no, no!" The passionate Frenchman placed his hands just below Kim's waist. "Seduce him with your hips!"

Kim choked back a laugh at the look on Aaron's face. Jacques was trying to teach the intricate moves of the sensual rumba. She and Aaron had mastered the footwork but were struggling to put the steps together with the overall movement of the dance.

"You love each other," Jacques grabbed Aaron's hand and put it on Kim's back. "That is crystal clarity." The French immigrant's misuse of American slang was endearing. "Stop the fear of showing it to Jacques!"

Kim was sure her lips would be bruised, since she was biting them to stop from laughing. She just nodded and turned her attention to the hip movement Jacques had demonstrated. Rumba was one of the sexiest Latin dances, according to Aaron who had researched the basic moves before their second class. He had not wanted to disappoint Monsieur Castille. 'Chemistry between the partners is necessary for a good rumba routine,' one website had stated.

"I'm not sure we're going to have enough 'chemistry' to master this one, honey," Aaron had whispered to Kim when Jacques finally moved on to another couple. After a grueling thirty minutes, their instructor called out to them from across the studio.

"Excellent, Miss Kim and Mr. Aaron," he called. Of course, it sounded like 'Mees Kim and Meester Air-own, but his praise was welcome.

"Thank you for the dance, Mees Kim." Aaron kissed Kim's hand with a flourish as they finished the dance.

"My pleasure, Monsieur Air-own," she replied.

On the way home, she couldn't help reliving the rumba lesson.

"The look on your face when Jacques was rocking my hips was priceless." Kim's laughter was hard to control. Aaron scowled.

"Yeah, I almost had to have a diplomatic discussion with our fine French friend over that move," Aaron said. "He should be glad that I understood it was simply part of his teaching style."

"His 'hands on' teaching style." Kim giggled at Aaron's returning frown.

As Aaron pulled into the parking lot of Kim's apartment complex, a slight dusting of snow was forming on the ground. Snow in this southern city was unusual but had been predicted for tomorrow. News and weather reports had been filled with little else over the last day.

"Looks like the weathermen got it right." Aaron zipped his jacket up when he got out of the car. "I hope it doesn't cause too many problems for business tomorrow."

"We don't have a lot going on, do we?" Kim asked. She was looking forward to the prospect of the wintery treat. Her college had been further north, and she had enjoyed the winter fun during her four years.

"No," Aaron said, "but I don't really want to deal with the hassle."

"Wow, who are you, and what have you done with my best friend?" Kim said. "I'm usually the one saying, 'no we can't do that' while I wrestle him to the floor before he can set the building on fire."

"Funny." He brushed away a snowflake that landed on her nose as he opened the passenger side door. "What do you suggest we do? Cancel work and make snowmen in the parking lot?"

"Could we?" Kim thought that was a great idea. If the snow hit as predicted many of their staff would not make it in. Just the threat of winter weather could cause the city to shut down.

"If it snows more than four inches," he conceded, "and is still on the ground by mid-morning, I'll let everyone go outside. We can have a snowball fight and snowman building contest." The meteorologists were predicting an inch of powdery flakes, at most. He wasn't likely to have to honor his promise.

"Four inches!" Kim knew that was unlikely. "That's not fair."

"Too bad," Aaron said. "You've rubbed off on me. I've become boring in my old age."

"Boring?" Kim knew Aaron was joking but pretended to be offended. "I'll show you! If it does snow enough, I'm going to use my first snowball to wipe that smug look off your handsome face!"

"Challenge accepted." Aaron walked her to her door, since the snow had indeed increased and the sidewalk was slick. She had taken off her high-heeled dance shoes and bare feet on a cold sidewalk meant the walk was more like a trot.

"Do you want some hot chocolate?" Kim offered as she unlocked her door.

"No, I'd better get home before it gets any worse," he said. "But hot chocolate sounds good. If we end up taking the snow break tomorrow, remind me and I'll get hot cocoa delivered from Lucy's Diner after our big battle."

***

The next morning, Aaron's phone a half hour before his alarm was set to ring.

"Have you looked outside?" Aaron rolled over and squinted at his alarm clock.

"Do you know what time it is?" Kim knew her call

would wake him up, but didn't care. The sight of five inches of snow on the ground in Atlanta was so rare that it was worth risking his displeasure.

An hour later, a quick call to the owner of the diner next door guaranteed hot drinks would be awaiting the office staff after their break. Mercer-Chem's downtown office was in an older part of the city that was undergoing a planned urban renewal. Lucy's was a mom-and-pop diner next door, which had survived the ups and downs of the economic rollercoaster that had affected many other businesses in the area.

Aaron was staring out the window at five inches of beautiful snow on the grounds. He could hear Kim in the office behind him, figuring out who was willing to stay behind to man the phones.

"I'm not going out in that weather!" Joyce said. "I'm too old to be frolicking during my morning break."

Kim was as like a little kid. Normally the calm, levelheaded member of the trio, Aaron was enjoying watching her enthusiasm. Of course, he pretended to be disappointed that he was wrong about the weather.

"I'm glad you were wrong." Kim poked her head into his office early that morning.

"Don't get used to it." Aaron's retort was quick. "It happens so rarely."

The half hour break began with a snowman-building contest and ended with the entire staff pelting their boss with snowballs as they ran for the cover of the building. Kim helped him brush off the powdery flakes before they headed inside.

"You're a mess," she teased. "Where did all this snow come from?"

"Traitor." Aaron laughed. "Was the attack planned all along or spontaneous? Who do I need to fire?"

The pair was enjoying their good-natured argument as they came through the lobby. Gigi stood in the door of the break room, sounds of the warming workers behind her.

"Gigi!" Aaron greeted his grimacing girlfriend. "You just missed all the fun!"

"I'm sure." Gigi's tone held a hint of impatience. "Did you forget our lunch date?"

"Uh, lunch?" Aaron's hesitation brought Kim to the rescue.

"He must've remembered." Kim reached up and began to tug off his coat. "I'm sure that's why he made us come in now. I wanted to stay out and play. Do you want some hot cocoa, Gigi? We figured everyone would need to warm up after our adventure. Feel free to grab a cup. I've got to take care of cleaning up our puddles so no one slips." Her babble gave Aaron a chance to recover.

"I'll grab my other coat and be ready in a jiffy." Aaron gave the impatient Gigi a quick kiss on the cheek. As he handed Kim the jacket he had shrugged off, he whispered, "You're my favorite."

"I know."

"I'll be back in an hour." Aaron checked in with Joyce

before leaving, and then turned to address the rosy-cheeked workers who were now enjoying their hot drinks. "No more playing! Back to work you people!" Laughter followed the couple out the door.

9

Tonight, We Tango

"How was lunch?" Kimberly asked as they pulled up to the dance studio that evening. "Did Gigi forgive you for forgetting?"

"Forgive me?" Aaron asked. "Of course! Your quick thinking worked. She didn't suspect anything. I owe you big time."

"I'll just add it to the list." Kim sighed. "You know it is exhausting being your best friend. What with the constant rescuing and wise advice and pampering I'm expected to provide."

"Ah, yes, but think how boring your life would be without me." Aaron tugged on her ponytail.

"True," she said. Jacques smiled as the laughing couple made their way into the mirrored studio.

"My favorites!" The Frenchman clapped and waved them over. "Tonight, we Tango!"

The couple learned the intricate dance quickly, despite

their struggle to maintain a small level of seriousness. Their dance master kept up a running soliloquy of romantic and dramatic scenarios to 'get you in the mood.' These ranged from a soldier returning home from war trying to win back his unfaithful wife, to a powerful man trying to seduce his reluctant secretary.

"I think Jacques watches too many soap operas." Kimberly could barely control her laughter as Aaron attempted a leer worthy of the nefarious boss.

"Maybe you should just pretend I'm Gigi and you're trying to convince me to forgive you for not remembering our lunch date." Kim batted her dark eyelashes at him. "That should be easy for your limited theatrical talent."

"Hilarious." Aaron frowned. "We'd be more successful if you pretended to be Gigi trying to get me into a compromising situation."

"Really?" Kim stumbled.

"Nothing I can't handle." Aaron quickly changed the subject. "Back to work! Here comes Monsieur Castille." Kim sighed dramatically as Aaron pulled her roughly against him, mimicking the example the master had shown at the beginning of the class.

"Fantastique!" Jacques praised. "You are most seducing and wonderfulness!" Kim buried her head against Aaron, hoping Monsieur couldn't hear her laughter.

At the end of the evening, Elinor passed out flyers to the dancers as they gathered their belongings. Every other Friday the studio had an open dance night. The class participants were encouraged to bring additional couples to share their newfound skills. There was a sign-up list to help the staff plan for the evening. They called in standby dancers to insure there would be an equal number of men and women present.

"Gigi's coming, right?" Kimberly asked as she signed her name, leaving the 'plus one' column blank. She would not be calling Scott.

"Yep." His response was less than enthusiastic. "Looks like you'll have to share me."

"I'll survive." Kim scanned down the names of those planning to attend. One of the older couples had entered the name 'Lt. Daniel Franklin' in the guest column.

"Hmm, looks like I'll be okay. The Franklins are bringing a soldier with them."

"Hopefully he won't be returning to an unfaithful girlfriend," Aaron glanced over her shoulder at the guest list.

"Maybe he knows how to rumba!" Kim's hopeful suggestion did not amuse Aaron.

"He'd better not!"

"You're no fun!" Kim poked Aaron as she moved past him to retrieve her coat from the row of chairs along the wall. "If you don't ever let me misbehave, you won't ever get me married off."

Kim had turned to pick up her coat, so she jumped as Aaron's arm came around her waist. She was unceremoniously hauled against his chest.

"Misbehaving is not the way to attract a man." His breath was warm on her cheek as he made his opinion clear. "I refuse to let you shake your hips to get a husband. Any man who would use that to his advantage will have to come through me."

"Relax, Aaron." She twisted away from him. "I was joking."

On the way home, their disagreement was forgotten as they laughed over Monsieur's attempts to motivate their 'mood' during the romantic dances. Kim was in tears as Aaron perfectly mimicked the accent.

"Be nice!" She gathered her shoes and gym bag from the back seat of the car. "Jacques is a sweetheart and you know it."

"I do." Aaron related how he knew Jacques had overheard his impersonation tonight and hadn't been upset.

"You have the accent patted down," the Frenchman had said, "but you must need the work on the attitude." He wasn't offended by Aaron's attempts and even managed to get a little dig in, too. "Maybe you perfect the French voice when you perfect the dances...or not!"

"Good for him!" Kim sighed.

"Tired?" Aaron asked as he opened her door. He reached across her and swung her legs out of the car. When he pulled her to her feet, she slipped her arms around his waist.

"Not tired, just sad." She rested her head against his chest. "I'm going to miss this." She sighed again and moved out of his arms.

"Miss what?" Aaron asked as they walked to the door.

"You, me, laughing. You know that when you get married, we won't be able to hang out like this anymore. I'm sure," she paused, refusing to say Gigi's name, "your future wife will not appreciate me as a third wheel."

She leaned her forehead against his chest once more before unlocking the door. "I'm just going to miss it. Goodnight, Aaron."

It was several minutes before she heard his car pull away.

10

A Very Scary Valentine

Aaron sighed as he watched his girlfriend join the conga line with her friends. The Valentine's Day charity event had been a lifesaver. The reprieve from having to take Gigi out for a romantic dinner tonight made the evening endurable—almost. Taking the opportunity that her distraction created, he slipped out to the terrace.

"Hey!" Kim's voice was slightly breathless. "What's up?"

"Are you okay? You sound winded." Aaron kept his eyes on the dancers inside, wanting to make sure Gigi didn't discover his absence. "What are you doing?"

"Well, right now, I'm picking up popcorn from the sofa, the floor, and my lap. The phone scared me."

"Don't tell me. You're watching a scary movie, aren't you?"

"Yes, dear heart. I figured it was the most appropriate choice for a lonely spinster on Valentine's Day." Kim paused the movie. "What are you doing calling me? Aren't you at some fancy shindig?"

"Yes, it's torture," Aaron said. "The only good thing is that the dance lessons have paid off. Gigi's mom was very impressed when I invited her to foxtrot."

"I'm glad." Kim picked up the last of the popcorn and settled back under her blanket. "So why did you call?"

"Just checking on you. I hate that you have to spend tonight alone," he said, "and you are not a spinster, my dear. I'll bet you had several offers for tonight that you turned down. Am I right?"

"Maybe," she said. "Spending tonight alone is not a big deal, though. You realize I usually spend this night alone, don't you? The last time I had a date on Valentine's Day was in high school, and that was the Sophomore Class dance. Remember Rodney?"

"I remember Rodney." Aaron noticed that the dance was ending and knew he needed to head back inside. "But I don't believe you haven't had a Valentine's date since then. We'll talk about this later, though. I've got to go."

"Okie dokie."

"Turn off that movie." Aaron heard the sounds of the scary music before he hung up. "You know you never sleep the night after you watch them and we have a big day at the office tomorrow."

"Whatever. Bye, Aaron."

He stared at the phone. She had hung up on him. He made it back to the table before Gigi did. She had stopped at the punch bowl and was downing her fourth or fifth cup. Aaron knew the concoction was spiked heavily and Gigi had the telltale signs of tipsiness.

"I've got a big day at the office tomorrow." Aaron pushed his cup of coffee toward her. "Would it be okay if we leave soon?"

"Really? It's so early, though." Gigi patted Aaron's coat pocket to locate his phone. As she pulled it out to check the time, he realized that his call to Kim had shown up on the screen. Despite her inebriation, Gigi's reaction was instantaneous.

"So, how's Kim?" She waved the phone under his nose, her words only slightly slurred.

"She's fine." Aaron snatched the phone from her hand. "I needed to check on something for work tomorrow. Like I said, we have a big day." Since he had actually mentioned work to Kim, he felt stretching the truth was justified.

"I'm going to stay, you go ahead and go. Mum and Dad will make sure I get home."

"Are you sure?" Aaron stood as he asked. Gigi shrugged her dismissal. He leaned over and kissed Gigi's upturned cheek. Twenty minutes later, he was knocking on Kim's door.

Wrapped in a blanket, her flannel pajama top and old sweatpants peaking out, Kim trudged to the door.

"Go away," she said as she hobbled back to the couch. "You're interrupting the important part. They just headed down to the basement. Stupid teenagers. Don't they know they're in a horror film? You never go into the basement!"

"Scoot over and hand me the popcorn." Aaron settled onto the recliner end of Kim's sofa after he grabbed a soda from the refrigerator. "I ordered pizza on my way over. It should be here any minute."

"Pizza? Didn't they feed you at that fancy shindig?"

"The theme was A Very Vegan Valentine."

"Ouch." Kim laughed at the grimace on Aaron's face. "You must be starving."

Aaron woke with a start at three in the morning. He was comfortably settled into Kim's reclining sofa, her fuzzy sock-covered feet in his lap. They had both fallen asleep halfway through the last dreadful movie. The plot of the film had centered on an alien sea creature eating his way through a seaside resort.

Glancing at the clock, Aaron decided to let Kim sleep where she was. He gently lifted her feet and slid off the sofa. She stirred when he tucked the blanket back around her legs.

"I fell asleep." She blinked up at him. "I never sleep after watching those movies. You must be magic."

"Yes, yes, I am." He leaned over and gave her a quick kiss on the forehead. "I'll see you in the morning. Love you."

"Love you, too."

11

Do You Rumba?

On Friday night, Kim decided to meet Aaron and Gigi at the studio, not wanting to intrude on their date night. She had taken off early and spent her free afternoon shopping. Inspired by the fun they had been having during the three weeks of dance lessons, she purchased a fancy ball gown that would be perfect for an upcoming charity event that Scott has asked her to attend, which was going to include dancing after dinner. Since she and Scott had remained friends, she was looking forward to the evening.

Tonight, she slipped on a simpler choice that she had found on sale at a second hand boutique. Knowing Gigi would be at the dance party, Kim paid extra attention to her style. Although Aaron's girlfriend had never said anything openly, Kim knew Gigi had a keen eye for fashion and sometimes had trouble hiding her opinion of fashion faux pas.

"You'll do." Kim spoke to her reflection. The silky material of the tea length dress swirled around her legs. It was perfect for dancing and its turquoise, blue, and green pattern gave her greenish brown eyes an exotic look. She was looking forward to the evening, especially since Elinor had called with the news that there were going to be plenty of young gentlemen available as dance partners.

The Franklins waved to her as she entered the studio. Their nephew was with them.

"Oh, my," Kim said under her breath as she caught sight of the handsome young Marine. Her expectations for enjoying the evening increased dramatically. Her broad smile was genuine as she was introduced to Lt. Franklin.

"This is our nephew, Daniel." Mrs. Franklin was glowing with pride. "He's on leave for the month and is making the rounds of his relatives."

"It's a pleasure to meet you, Daniel." Kim couldn't help but admire the broad shoulders, dreamy brown eyes, and close-cropped dark hair. "I hope you haven't been forced into dance service against your will." She shot a grin to his uncle.

"Oh no, Miss Calhoun," the young man assured her. "My ROTC program commander required that we learn to waltz. I think it was due to the fact that his wife was a fan of ballroom dancing."

"Well, it's a skill that will serve you well, I'm sure."

Kim smiled up him. "You'll be in high demand tonight," she added, hoping he would take the bait. "And please call me Kim."

"May I have the honor of the first waltz, Kim?" He grinned, not fooled at all by her not so subtle hint.

"Why, yes, Daniel." Kim curtsied. "It would be my pleasure." The two new friends were still sharing a laugh as Aaron and Gigi approached. Kim hadn't noticed their arrival.

"Daniel, I'd like you to meet my friends." Kim made the introductions with a smile, despite Aaron's frown. "This is Aaron Mercer and Gigi Peterson. Aaron has endured dance lessons with me these past two weeks and is anxious to show Gigi all that he's learned."

"Nice to meet you, Lt. Franklin." Aaron sized up the young officer. Gigi did as well, a fact not lost on Aaron. "Where are you stationed?"

"I'm heading to Camp Lejeune next month and will be deploying sometime mid-summer. I'm using my leave to visit extended family." Daniel winked at his aunt. "Then I'll be spending the last couple of weeks in my hometown."

"Is that nearby?" Gigi patted the soldier's muscular bicep.

"Yes, just an hour upstate." The lieutenant blinked as the full force of Gigi's charm was directed toward him.

"Lovely." Gigi slipped her arm through his and led him to a chair.

"You'd better go rescue him." Aaron nodded toward

his girlfriend as she led the young soldier away.

"My pleasure." Kim smoothed the skirt of her dress and quickly followed the couple. She caught the smile of thanks from Mrs. Franklin, but missed Aaron's scowl.

"Gigi, Aaron has a dance card for you." Kim joined Gigi and her latest prey. "They're going to make it easy for us to keep track of our dance partners. Here, Daniel, you need to pencil in the waltz on my card."

A slightly inelegant huff came from Gigi as she returned to Aaron's side.

"Sorry about that. Please tell me you have a girlfriend, or better yet a wife." Kim slid into the chair Gigi vacated. "That may be what it takes to ward her off." Sometimes she wondered why Aaron continued to put up with Gigi's antics.

"Yes, ma'am, I do have a girlfriend." The tension that Kim sensed as Gigi dragged him away a few minutes early evaporated as he confided this news. "I'm actually hoping to propose next week."

"Wonderful!" Kim hugged him spontaneously. "Well, I'm going to flirt outrageously with you tonight, so be warned. That should keep the sharks away. Or at least one of them. Does that sound like a good plan?"

"Worthy of the best military minds," Daniel said. Their laughter garnered another scowl from Aaron and secret smiles from several other classmates.

"You don't happen to know how to rumba, do you?" Kim couldn't resist the temptation.

"Yes, I do." Daniel's answer surprised her. "I'm not

sure that would be appropriate in my dress uniform, though. I'll have to stick to the calmer dances."

"I understand," Kim said. "How about a tango?"

Aaron was heading their way. She wanted to have her ammunition ready before he claimed any dances.

"I could do that." Daniel grinned, writing in his name for the first and last waltz, and the tango that was scheduled right before their refreshment break. He could see that there was some sort of friendly combat going on between Aaron and Kim. He raised an eyebrow in question.

"Aaron's my best friend," Kim whispered quickly. "He's a little overprotective."

"Not violent, is he?"

"Only if you poke him with a stick," she said, not even cracking a smile. Daniel's bark of laughter caused Aaron's frown to deepen, which only caused the two new friends to break out in another round of childish chuckles.

"Kim." Aaron's tone was strained. "Did you happen to save any dances for your *dance partner*?"

"Rumba?" Kim couldn't resist. Daniel almost choked on the sip of water he had just taken. "Or will you save that for Gigi?" She decided she had pushed Aaron enough.

"I think Jacques will expect us to attempt one," Aaron said, deflecting the responsibility for his request, "as well as a tango. Are you up for a foxtrot, too?"

"We didn't master that one, you know." Kim had

finally gotten her humor back under control.

"I'll put my name down for it. We can always sit it out if we want." He took his time with her card, noting the three dances Daniel had reserved.

"I guess I need to make the rounds if I want to spread the love around." Kim heard a growl and a laugh behind her. She moved away, looking for Mr. Franklin and Monsieur Jacques so she could get them on her list.

12

Are You Writing a Book?

Kim and Daniel made a striking couple on the dance floor. She was impressed with the officer's skill and praised him as they headed back to their chairs after the first waltz.

"Your future wife is a lucky lady." Kim patted his arm with one hand and used her dance card to fan her flushed face with the other. The studio wisely planned short breaks in-between the dances, knowing the dancers would need a chance to catch their breath. Kim glanced at her card and saw that Aaron was her next partner so was not surprised to see him dragging Gigi towards them.

"Here come our next partners." Kim sighed. "Are you ready?"

"I'll make sure I bring up the girlfriend information right away," Daniel said. "Is that acceptable, ma'am?"

"Perfect, Lt. Franklin." Kim executed a perfect salute.

Once again, their laughs seemed to displease one of the pair that had just joined them.

"Are you enjoying yourself?" Aaron's tone matched his frown. "Is Sgt. Swanky treating you well?"

"Sgt. Swanky? Do you mean Lt. Luscious?" Kim sighed and fanned herself playfully with her dance card. Seeing Aaron's frown, she shook her finger at him. "You're being childish."

"And you drooling over the majestic Marine is *not* childish?" Aaron snapped.

"Keep your voice down, dear." Kim smiled sweetly. "You're turning a little green around the edges. You should be more upset about your girlfriend making eyes at the dashing lieutenant." Aaron shrugged indifferently.

"Don't worry, though. Daniel has a girlfriend, who is soon to be his fiancée. Her name is Laura Harper. So breathe, please, Aaron. You're killing my hand with your grip." Kim rubbed her fingers when he released them.

"Sorry." His pout lessened. "You still should tone it back some. I'm sure Laura wouldn't appreciate the batting eyelashes."

"Mine or Gigi's?" Kim's remark earned a reluctant grin.

"Touché," Aaron said.

***

During the light buffet, Daniel and the Franklins invited Kim to sit with them. Aaron and Gigi were cornered by Monsieur Castille who had learned Gigi was fluent in French. Aaron's longsuffering countenance would have been funny if Kim didn't feel a bit sorry for him.

"Laura just sent me a message." Daniel settled himself in the seat next to Kim. "She got someone to cover for her this weekend, so she'll be in town tomorrow."

"That's great!" Kim kept her voice quiet, not knowing if Daniel's aunt and uncle were aware of his plans. "Do you have a ring yet? Are you going to surprise her or is she going to help pick it out?"

"Yes, yes, and no," Daniel answered. "I told her where I was tonight and she'd like to go dancing tomorrow night."

"That should be fun," Kim said between bites of a delicious lobster puff. "Maybe you can teach her some of the new moves you've learned tonight."

"I was actually going to ask you a favor," Daniel said. "She's dragging her older brother Mitchell with her. He'll be one of the groomsmen. Would you like to join us for dinner and help with the dance lessons?"

"Hmm, let me think." Kim tapped her cheek. "Dinner with two handsome men, meeting a lovely young lady, and another evening of dancing? I think I could bring myself to endure it."

"Perfect!" Daniel said, just as Aaron came up behind Kim to claim her for their foxtrot. "I'll pick you up at six." He stood and shook Aaron's hand as Kim cleared her place.

"Pick you up at six? You're going on a date with

him?" Aaron swung Kim onto the dance floor.

"Yes, Warden Mercer." Kim teased him when the movement of the dance allowed her to speak. "Shall I ask him to seek your permission?"

"I thought you said he had a girlfriend."

"He does." Their conversation mimicked the rhythm of the dance.

"Does she know about his plans tomorrow night?"

"You're being awfully nosy," she said as he continued to frown. "Are you writing a book?"

"Why are you avoiding the question?"

"Why are you asking the question?"

Aaron fell quiet as they concentrated on the graceful dance. They hadn't perfected it by any means but followed Jacques and Elinor's movements well enough to keep from stumbling. As the music ended, Aaron pulled Kim close and tilted her chin up to meet his gaze.

"Be careful, Kimmie," he said quietly. "Don't play with the man's affections." Kim realized she had pushed her best friend a little too far.

"Thank you, Aaron." Kim kissed his cheek gently. "I promise it will be fine. Laura knows." As they moved off the dance floor, Kim saw that Gigi was watching them. "I'll go smooth out Gigi's furrowed brow."

"Thanks." Aaron led Kim to the chairs along the mirrored wall before seeking out his next partner. "Let her know that my next dance is with Elinor, but that we can leave after that. Love you."

"Love you, too, dearest." Kim patted his arm before

finding Gigi.

"Fine." Gigi's clipped response to Aaron's message relayed through Kim meant Aaron was in for a rough ride home.

"Thanks for letting him take these lessons with me, Gigi." Kim hoped she could smooth things over for Aaron. "I was more shaken than I admitted over Scott breaking up with me and this was the perfect tonic."

Her sincere words seemed to soothe Aaron's girlfriend. Monsieur Jacques claimed her for the next dance. Kim checked her dance card and realized that Aaron's early departure meant he would miss their rumba.

"Coward." She mouthed, pointing to her dance card as she caught his eye across the room. His salute confirmed her suspicions.

13

May I Cut In?

Laura Harper's brother Mitchell was indeed a good-looking man. *This is certainly giving me the hope I needed when I was despairing*, Kim thought. She was glad she had chosen one of her most attractive outfits. The long silky maroon blouse paired with slender dress jeans and trendy boots rivaled even Gigi's fashion choices. Kim had worn a favorite necklace, too, but had hesitated over the accessory. The gold chain with a garnet pendant hung lower that she had expected. After several minutes of buttoning and unbuttoning, she finally decided that leaving one extra button undone was not too provocative. Compared to the amount of skin Aaron's girlfriend usually exposed, Kim was dressed like a Puritan.

The new friends enjoyed a delicious dinner at a fancy steak house, an innovative restaurant that specialized in traditional dishes with an upscale twist. Elegant decorations were interspersed with quirky antiques. Kim knew she'd be gloating to the Courtney and Geoff tomorrow. They had talked about visiting the fancy hot spot as soon as baby Abigail was old enough to stay with a babysitter.

A large dance floor next to the bar featured a live band known for its eclectic music. This meant the bar attracted a wide range of patrons. At any given point in the evening, the band could be playing Latin dance tunes, country songs for line dances, or modern pop songs. Daniel and Laura were looking forward to learning some new dance moves. Mitchell not so much.

Kim and Daniel demonstrated a simplified tango as the brother and sister watched from a table at the edge of the dance floor. Mitchell provided a running humorous commentary that kept his sister in stitches. Daniel's glare was unconvincing since he was laughing just as much as they were.

The band assisted the impromptu lessons and played another tango-friendly number. Daniel and Kim spent the time describing the moves to Laura and Mitch, and even took the pair into the hallway to practice a couple times through the tricky parts. More laughter ensued as other patrons watched the young couples.

During a country two-step, a dance Mitch and Laura knew well, Kim and Daniel followed behind them, trying to match their moves. The band decided to give the dancers a taste of their ever-changing playlist and the next number was a slow-paced waltz. Mitch and Kim laughingly waved the other two back onto the floor.

"We're exhausted," Kim said. "Daniel, you don't need any help on your waltz. We'll admire your expertise from here."

"This has been fun." Mitchell motioned to the waiter for a refill on their sodas. "Thanks for being such a good sport."

"My pleasure, Officer Harper." Kim fanned her headed cheeks with one of the menus. "Laura told me you were a rising star in your precinct. You're coming back down this week to interview locally, is that right?" Mitchell had just passed his detective exam and was applying for a position here in the city.

"Great detective work, Miss Calhoun." Mitchell saluted her with his newly delivered drink. "I'm glad you're not competing with me for the position!"

The next tune was another slow song, so Kim and Mitchell joined the other couples on the dance floor. Kim was having such a good time she didn't see the newcomers at their table. Halfway through the dance, Daniel and Mitchell switched partners. As they swirled through a turn, Kim's eyes widened as Aaron appeared behind Daniel.

"May I cut in?" His voice made it clear that he expected an affirmative answer.

"Aaron!" Kim's breathless response caused Daniel to hesitate.

"Kim?" Daniel asked. She shook her head against the muddle of questions his sudden appearance created.

"No?" Aaron's brows shot up.

"No. I mean, yes," she stammered. "It's fine." Daniel handed her over to Aaron, giving her hand a reassuring squeeze before joining Mitchell and Laura who had returned to the table.

"What are you doing here?" Kim's brow furrowed.

"Dancing."

"You know what I mean." Kim twisted to look over her shoulder. "Where's Gigi? Does she know you're stalking me and Daniel?"

"So, it's 'me and Daniel' now, is it?" Aaron asked. Kim stepped on his foot.

"Ouch." Aaron pulled his foot out of her reach in case there was a second rebuke. "She's at the table. Adonis caught her eye."

"How did you know he was with us?" Kim knew any interrogation would have to be done while they were dancing.

"Gigi recognized your purse. She said it was a girl thing." Aaron explained as he moved to where he could see their table. "Who is the Roman god? Another conquest?"

"Adonis is Greek," Kim said. "You shouldn't have slept through Mrs. Grandlin's mythology lectures." Sophomore year's Global studies class had been one of their favorites. "Your description is accurate for sure, though." She sighed for effect. "He's Laura's brother. His name is Mitchell, but I heard Daniel call him Mitch."

"Married?" Aaron asked. Kim frowned up at him.

What is his problem?

"No," she said. "Would you like me to warn him away from Gigi? Or encourage him?" A false smile accompanied her offer.

"Hilarious." Aaron bowed over her hand as the dance ended. "Thank you for the dance. Shall we join the others?"

"Absolutely, that would be lovely." Kim curtsied and pasted on a smile. "I can think of nothing else that would make this evening more enjoyable."

"Lies with a hint of sarcasm." Aaron's breath brushed her cheek as he bent his head bent close to her ear. "And here I was thinking the restaurant only served steak and seafood."

Kim watched Gigi's attention turn toward them. The young debutante had claimed Mitch's arm but was zoned in on her boyfriend's behavior at the same time. Kim wondered what game Aaron was playing.

Introductions were made as the group sat out the next dance. All six joined in for a Latin line dance, and when the band started the strains of another tango, Kim pulled a reluctant Mitch onto the floor and picked a spot close to Daniel and Laura. The night was intended to teach them the moves, so Kim ignored Aaron's frown as he sat pacifying his pouting girlfriend.

When the next song was a country number, Kim spoke quietly to Mitchell. The handsome man nodded and led a willing Gigi onto the floor as Kim settled into the redhead's vacant stool.

"Finally, some privacy. I need to speak to you." Kim's clenched jaw was a warning as she and Aaron watched the other four dance a country two-step.

"Yes, Your Highness," Aaron said, half his attention on the plate of appetizers Daniel had just ordered. "What have I done now?

"Well," Kim said, wavering between bluntness and all out attack. "What on earth is wrong with you!" The punch that accompanied her words got his attention.

"Ouch!" He rubbed his upper arm. "That hurt!"

"Poor baby." Kim's tone was evidence that she felt anything but sympathy for him. "You're acting like a child."

"And you're acting like a..." Aaron started and then stopped suddenly. He rubbed the back of his neck.

"A what?" Kim moved the snacks out of his reach. "If you even vaguely insinuate that I'm acting inappropriately, I may hit you again, only harder this time."

"Does Marvelous Mitchell know that you just dumped your last boyfriend a couple weeks ago?" Aaron avoided her gaze and retrieved the platter.

"Now you're being obnoxious," Kim said. "If I didn't love you so much, I would ask you to leave." She sighed. "Oh, and thanks for the reminder, although you got it wrong. Scott broke up with me, remember?"

"Sorry," he said.

"Besides, Mr. Hoity Toity," she continued, "this evening was meant to teach Mitch and Laura some fun dance moves for the wedding. The wedding that she doesn't know Daniel has planned already. He's going to propose this week."

Aaron sat quietly, letting her rant. His bowed head implied that he knew he deserved her censure.

"Grow up, Aaron," she said, reaching for her purse. "Why you feel the freedom, or need, to butt into my relationship issues I don't understand."

"I care about you."

"This is why it's so unfair that I'm not allowed to do the same. What makes you think I care any less about you?" Kim's outburst silenced Aaron so she continued. "I'm not interested in Officer Harper. For one thing, I've just come out of a relationship and I'm not looking for another one. Secondly, for some reason I'm not at all attracted to him." She took a shaky breath. "And thirdly, he may be a nice guy, but I don't know if we share the same values."

Aaron twirled the straw in his drink distractedly. Afraid she had lost his attention she pulled his chin around to face her. He needed to know she was serious.

"I've invited them to church tomorrow, but I'm not sure they'll want to come now," she said, her gaze now boring into him.

"Why not?" Aaron frowned.

"Unfortunately, they know that you'll be there."

14

Definitely Not Gigi

Kim had been planning a trip to the ladies' room so she escaped after delivering her lecture. She stomped off, blinking back tears of anger. Aaron caught up with her in the hallway, away from the sight of the others.

"Your behavior tonight has been anything but welcoming." Kim admonished him as she moved toward the ladies' room.

"I'm sorry." Aaron blocked her progress and turned her to face him, his arm lightly grasping her elbow. "I'll make a deal with you. I'll try to behave if you'll do something for me." He positioned himself to her prevent her escape.

"What?" Her eyes were still bright from the tears she was fighting.

"You're not going to like my request, but please understand I'm not saying this because I'm mad." Aaron ran his hands down her arms and grasped her hands. "You are right about my attitude."

"Just tell me, Aaron." Kim closed her eyes as he tugged her closer.

"Please button up your blouse." Aaron spoke quietly in her ear. Kim's eyes flew open.

"What? You're crazy!" She backed away and covered the skin above her blouse with shaking hands. "Compared to the other ladies in the room, my outfit is practically Victorian!"

"You, Miss Calhoun, are not every other lady in the room!" Aaron insisted. Kim's fuming eyes let him know her opinion of his opinion.

"What about Gigi?" She forced herself to speak quietly. The unfairness of his double standard made her want to shout at him. His arms folded in challenge as she started to argue.

"You, my dear, are definitely not Gigi." Aaron reached for her again but she leaned away. He dropped his hands. "Just do it, Kim."

"Fine." She smirked at him. Fingering the four open buttons, she fastened them slowly, one by one, all the way up. To close the last one, Kim had to lift her chin. "How's that?"

"Now who's being childish?" His frustration was clear as he unbuttoned the top three buttons. He brushed her long dark hair back over her shoulder and tilted her chin up with one finger.

Neither of them had seen the slightly inebriated

gentleman who had stumbled out of the men's room.

"Get a room, you two." The intoxicated patron's slurred words were accompanied by a pat on Aaron's back. Kim gasped. Aaron stepped back quickly as he saw the blush cross her cheeks. The man's companion grabbed him as he swayed.

"Sorry," the younger man said. "We're just leaving."

"I'll attempt to be a gentleman the rest of the evening," Aaron said. "I'm not promising I'll be perfect, but I'll try to stop the pouting." He turned and stalked back to the table.

Laura found Kim in the ladies' room a few moments later, staring at her reflection in the mirror.

"I was wondering where you disappeared to," Laura said. "Everything okay?"

"Yes." Kim had buttoned and unbuttoned the blouse's top four buttons several times. "How does this look? Can you still see my necklace? Aaron objected to the amount of skin I was displaying." Normally Kim would keep her private disagreements private, but she was still smarting from his lecture. "I think he was retaliating because I told him he was being rude. I hope he's not made the evening unpleasant for you guys."

"Oh, no." Laura nodded as Kim adjusted her necklace, and then turned to touch up her lipstick. "Whatever you said to him helped. He was all rainbows and sunshine when we got back to the table."

"That, I can picture!" Kim smoothed out the blouse one last time and the two women rejoined their party, laughing at the idea of Aaron Mercer leaping around the room with a basket of pastel rainbows and sunshine.

Any uninvolved bystander would say the group managed to enjoy themselves for the rest of the evening. Kim was miserable. What seemed like hours later, Daniel's group said their goodbyes. Kim hugged Laura warmly and promised to keep in touch.

"You're close enough, so we should get together soon," Kim said, trying not to reveal that she knew Daniel was going to propose this week. "We'll go shopping, or better yet, pretend to go shopping and just go out for cheesecake!"

Laura laughed and then moved off with Daniel. The couple had silently agreed to encourage Mitch to walk Kim to her car. For some reason Gigi seemed to have a different idea. The auburn beauty captured Mitch's attention, and his arm, as they left the bar. Aaron scowled and joined Kim as they stepped into the parking lot.

"You're going to get wrinkles if you keep frowning." Kim patted his arm as they walked to her car. Aaron's mood did not respond to her teasing. Confused and exhausted from the physical and emotional activity of the evening, Kim decided to do what she wanted, whether or not Aaron approved. "I'm going to go reclaim Mitch." She turned and followed Mitch and Gigi.

"Mitch!" Kim called and saw the look of relief on his face as he gently detangled himself from Gigi's grip. Aaron had followed Kim across the parking lot, so he intervened.

"Gigi, let's give these two some privacy," Aaron said, moving his girlfriend away. He gave Kim a quick nod. "See you tomorrow."

"Thank you," Mitch said. As Aaron and Gigi moved away, he asked the question that had been on his mind all evening. "What's up with those two?"

"Oh, you know." Kim shrugged and waved toward the couple. "Gigi's one of a kind."

"You can say that again," he said, as they walked back to Kim's car. "So, if I call and ask you to help me find my way around town if I get the job, would you hang up on me?"

"Smooth, Officer Harper." Kim laughed as she fumbled in her purse for her keys. "You know I just got out of a relationship and I'm not looking for another one."

"Yes, but you would take pity on a poor, lonely bachelor, right?" Mitchell grabbed her hand and raised it to his lips. Aaron's car engine revved. "Aaron saw that, didn't he?"

Kim leaned around Mitchell and frowned at Aaron as he drove slowly past them.

"Wow. That was a powerful glare. I'm glad I didn't try anything more. He probably would have wrecked his car."

"True." Kim gave him a quick hug and then slid into her driver's seat.

"You explained Gigi, but what's up with Aaron?"

"Best friend," she said simply.

"Gigi's?" Mitch asked in confusion.

"No." Kim smiled faintly. "Mine." The look on Mitch's face was priceless.

The sounds of the opening hymn were ending the next morning as Aaron slid into the pew next to Kim. She scooted over several inches.

"Still mad at me?" He took the hymnal from her hands and slipped his arm along the pew behind her.

"Should I be?" She batted her eyes at him. A smile broke out across his handsome face and he nodded.

During the greeting time, Aaron apologized once more for his behavior. Neither of them mentioned his actions in the parking lot.

"I was a boor and you were gracious to not kick me out of the restaurant last night," he said.

"Agreed," she said.

"I see Michael-Marshall-Maxwell didn't make it today." Aaron looked around the sanctuary. "Too bad."

"It's Mitchell, and you know it." She tried to hide her smile. "They had to get back home. I'll let you know when he's going to be in town, though, if you like. Maybe you two can hang out." Her offer was accompanied by a wide smile.

"Funny," he said.

"Even better," she suggested as the congregation returned to their seats for the sermon, "you and Gigi could join Mitchell and me for a double date."

15

The New Accountant

Kim trudged into the office. Today was the first day of the major financial audit. Aaron had been in a bad mood for several days, which had made the prospect of the fiscal project even less appealing.

"You'll never believe who's standing in my office." Aaron's voice came over the intercom. For the first time in over a week, he sounded cheerful. "Our new accountant is going to make your day." Kim gathered the files for the meeting, now looking forward to the tedious audit more than before.

"Chip!" Kim dropped the stack of files on Aaron's coffee table and hugged the newcomer warmly. Chip Larson was one of her best friends from high school. They had served as editors on the school yearbook and had almost all their classes together their senior year. Chip was voted Best Sense of Humor that year. It was an almost unanimous vote. His humor made him extremely popular, a status that was unusual for a guy whose height put him eye to eye with most of the females in the class. He was Kim's exact height and they shared identical coloring. These similarities meant many people—including teachers—had thought they were brother and sister.

"My long-lost sister!" Chip held her at arms length. "You're as beautiful as ever! Not surprising, though, since you and I share our magnificent looks."

"It's the genes," Kim said. "Do you think Mrs. Locke has forgiven us?" The pair had gone the entire fall semester of their junior year letting their Physics teacher think they were fraternal twins.

"How she believed us was always beyond me," Chip said. "The whole line we fed her about our parents splitting up and you taking on our mom's maiden name. Wow. I still feel a little guilty."

"We were terrible, true, but it was hilarious at the time." Kim finally turned to Aaron. "Did you know he was our new accountant?"

"Nope." Aaron held up Chip's business card. "I had no idea 'Charles Larson, CEO of Larson Accounting' was in fact our good friend here."

"This is going to be such fun." Kim and Chip sat at the conference table, files and spreadsheets neatly arranged. "How will we ever get anything done? I'm sure the rest of the office will get tired of our laughter."

"My goal in life is to show people that accounting is the most exciting profession there is." Chip smiled at

Kim. "I'm sure you'll agree before this is over."

As they worked through the audit, the two friends caught up on what had been going on in each of their lives over the last few years. Chip was single, too, a fact he humorously injected into the middle of the August report.

"Speaking of cost overrun," he said, "why aren't either of us married yet? Has the world gone crazy?"

"Crazy, or clueless." Kim laughed. "They just don't know what they're missing!"

"Seriously, though, Kim, why aren't you and Aaron married yet?"

"Well, he's been dating someone for a few months, but we don't talk about his love life. Me? I still haven't found someone that can put up with me!"

"No, I mean, why haven't you married each other? I always thought you'd end up together."

"Me and Aaron? Oh, no!" Kim was glad she hadn't taken a sip of her soda since she was sure she would have choked. "When I first showed up in middle school, I had a huge crush on him, but soon realized he was way out of my league. I think Courtney would have warned me away, anyway."

"Warned you away? She didn't want you dating him?"

"Maybe not warned me away, but I know she was glad I got over my infatuation. She wanted us all to be good friends and knew that bringing romance into the mix would mess that up."

Neither of the two friends had heard Aaron approach the conference room. He had stopped outside the door when he heard Chip mention his name. He turned on his heel and went back to his office so he missed the rest of the conversation.

"Sounds like you guys are more like siblings." Chip said.

"Siblings?" Kim tapped the table with her pencil. "No, not really. It's different. Deeper, I think. He's my best friend. He drives me crazy but I couldn't live without him either."

"Sounds pretty special," Chip said.

"Yes, it is," Kim said. "I trust him more than anyone. Actually, I think I'd trust Aaron to pick out a husband for me."

"Wow! That's profound."

"I know, right? But it'd save me a lot of trouble!"

***

The audit and preparations for next year's projections took several days. Friday night came and they were still working when Aaron ventured toward the conference room—a room he had avoided all week.

"Everyone else is gone." Aaron stood in the doorway. "Are you guys going to get done tonight?"

"Just finished." Kim was stacking the files neatly and Chip was entering the last numbers into his laptop.

"Dinner?" Aaron asked, nodding to both, but looking directly at Kim, almost rudely ignoring Chip.

"No thanks," she said. "Chip's going to wine and dine me. He says I'm a natural at this number stuff. I think he wants to lure me to the dark side." Chip grinned.

"She's mine, Charles," Aaron said. "This place would fall apart without her."

"Got it, big guy." Chip wasn't fooled by the light tone of Aaron's last comment. He had seen the Aaron's fist tightened on the door jamb.

An hour later, Chip and Kim were finishing their meal. As the waitress refilled their coffee cups one more time, Chip broached the subject of Mr. Aaron Mercer once more.

"So, what is Aaron's girlfriend like?"

"Oh, you know the type." Kim shrugged. "Beautiful, classy, rich. You've probably even heard of her. He's been dating Gigi Peterson since November."

"Gigi Peterson? As in the New York Peterson's?" Chip's eyebrow shot up. "That's pretty high company."

"Gigi's dad and Uncle Larry are fraternity brothers. It's weird, though, because they couldn't be less alike." Kim finished the delicious chocolate lava cake that Chip had insisted she order. "I think Aaron's dad reluctantly agreed to the relationship when Aaron pointed out it could help the business in the long run."

"Are they serious?"

"As close as Aaron and I are, we don't discuss Gigi." Kim folded her napkin neatly and placed it on her plate. Chip understood the subject was closed so he changed the topic back to work, making plans to return next month after Aaron's round of new product conferences. Decisions would need to be made for new or different suppliers, as well as about adding any new lines.

As they pulled back into the office parking lot, returning Kim to her car, the two friends made plans to go out again. During dinner, Chip had revealed that he was pursuing a long-distance relationship with a girl he had dated in college. They had ended their relationship at graduation but had reconnected at a recent alumni event.

"It will be nice to have a friend to go out with, without the awkwardness of a romantic relationship," Kim said. "Besides, it would be kind of weird being in a relationship with someone who looks like he could be my brother."

"Yes, but think how good looking our kids would be!"

16

The Savannah Rule

End of the quarter inventory kept the whole office busy for several days. Aaron left a week later for an eco-friendly products conference in California.

"Courtney better not have that baby while I'm gone," he said as Kim dropped him off at the airport. They had both been so busy that they had not spent any time together outside of the office since the dance party. Aaron seemed preoccupied, but Kim attributed it to the inventory issues, and his pending trip.

"I'll be sure to let her know your orders," Kim pushed the button to pop open her trunk as he got out of the car. "She's not due for a couple of weeks, so you should be fine."

"Good." He leaned through the open window and gave her a quick kiss on the cheek. "Try not to miss me too much and please try to behave while I'm gone!"

"I will if you will, mister." She realized how much she had missed his grin over the last couple of weeks. As he walked around the car to hand his luggage to the baggage handler, she rolled down the passenger window.

"Aaron, have a good time, okay?" She blew him a kiss when he turned around, then added, "Love you." Aaron simply nodded.

Joyce noticed Kim's pensive mood when she returned from the airport.

"What's going on with you and Aaron?" Joyce asked Kim over their salads at lunch. Lucy's was too crowded, so they had picked up their orders to go and were eating in the break room.

"What do you mean?" Kim had thought she had hidden her concerns better, but Joyce was an astute observer. "He has been a little off the last couple of weeks, but he's always a little off, though, right?"

"True," Joyce said. "How was he when you dropped him off this morning?"

"Back to his old self, for the most part." Kim hoped her assurances sounded convincing. "A few days after our dance lessons ended, we had a misunderstanding, which I thought we had fixed after church that Sunday. But that Monday he was in a funk again."

"I remember. I was glad he had to spend most of that week at the plant with his dad."

"Me, too," Kim said. "Whatever it was I'm sure he would have talked to Courtney or me about it if it was important. She hasn't said anything, though."

"Let's hope this week away will give him a chance to relax some, too. He's done an amazing job getting this branch established. I'm glad his dad is so supportive, too."

"Uncle Larry and Aunt Gina are great," Kim said. Aaron's parents were exceptional people. When tragedy struck, Courtney's dad had leaned heavily on both Larry and Gina, not knowing how to handle his own grief and that of his children. Courtney's brother Allen was older, already married, and out of the house. Although Allen missed his mom and the influence she would have had on his children, Courtney's sorrow was more acute. She would have had a more difficult recovery if Gina had not stepped in, putting aside her own grief to be there for her best friend's daughter.

"They raised three very fine children." Joyce sipped the last of her diet soda. Aaron's younger brother Ben and sister Amanda were in college. Ben was finishing his freshman year, still deciding whether to major in Chemistry or Communications. Amanda was graduating this semester with a degree in Elementary Education.

"Well..." Kim drew a laugh. "Two out of three isn't bad."

"Speaking of the bad, we haven't seen Gigi in a while." Joyce didn't hide her feelings very well.

"Please don't go there, Joyce," Kim said. "You know that I've worked hard to be nice to Aaron's latest paramour. There are times when she's sweet and friendly, and others when she could be the poster child for single, privileged rich girls. I haven't quite figured her out."

"Well, you know my opinion of their relationship," Joyce said as she washed out her glass and placed it on the drying rack. "I've made sure that Aaron knows he needs to be careful. Ms. Georgiana is much too ambitious for my taste."

"I'm trying to stay out of it!" Kim raised her hands in surrender. "I learned my lesson long ago," she added. "Not going to go there again, that's for sure."

"Again?" Joyce's curiosity stopped her at the door of the break room. "Sounds like the voice of experience. Pray tell, missy."

"It was no big deal," Kim said. "Just a stupid childish trick that almost ended our friendship." There was no use trying to pass the long-ago incident off as insignificant. Memories of it always brought a wave of regret.

"What on earth did you do?" Joyce asked. She couldn't think of anything horrific enough to come between Aaron and Kimberly.

"First, I was only fifteen, so I'm going to plead partial insanity," Kim said. Trying to paint the memory in a funny light may help ease the pain of the confession. "It was sophomore year, and Aaron was dating a girl that Courtney and I didn't really like. He broke his hand a couple weeks into the baseball season. The first day he returned to school with his cast, I slathered on the reddest lipstick you've ever seen and laid a big kiss on it. Savannah was furious. So was Aaron."

"How did he not know what you were doing?" Joyce was laughing at the picture Kim's story painted.

"It wasn't funny." Kim wagged her finger at the older lady. "I convinced him to close his eyes while I "signed" his cast, pretending that I didn't want him to read what I was writing." She could feel the blush of shame, even almost ten years later. "I didn't think he would ever forgive me. He had the baseball trainer wrap an ace bandage over his cast."

"So, you vowed to never interfere again?" Joyce now understood why she had never heard Kim disparage Gigi. Her comment earlier about spoiled rich girls was the most Kim had ever revealed about her true feelings.

"Right you are," Kim said. "I call it the Savannah Rule. Courtney can express her opinion, in guarded terms, at the beginning of his relationships. The only major objection I can voice is concern over the lady not sharing his spiritual values."

"Have you ever questioned his relationship with Gigi?"

"Not to his face." Kim sighed as she cleaned up her lunch dishes. "I'm sure he knows how I feel, though. I'm not very good at hiding my feelings from Aaron. Unless I find out Gigi's a serial killer, or already married, or doesn't like chocolate,"—she shivered at the thought—"I'm staying out of this one!"

"You sure you two are all right, though?" Joyce pressed the issue she had raised earlier. Kim only nodded, glancing over her shoulder with a smile.

***

Two days later, inventory was done. Kim had the last of several conference calls with Aaron's dad making projections for the next year and going over the numbers Chip and she had run. Having an office in the city had the advantages of being closer for the salesmen, who could now stop by for samples, and no longer had to trek two hours up the interstate to the factory.

"My dear, I think this experiment has turned out better than we expected," Aaron's dad said. "You and my son have done a marvelous job this year."

"It's been fun, Uncle Larry," Kim said, then changed the subject. "How's Aunt Gina holding up? I know the baby isn't due for another month, but she's got to be getting excited."

"Oh, yes!" Larry sighed. "If Courtney doesn't have little Abigail soon our extra bedroom will officially become a baby supply store. My wife keeps finding 'just one more thing' for her new niece."

"Courtney can't wait, either," Kim said. "She's miserable. I told her that it could be worse and she could've been suffering through her last month in the middle of July!" Kim didn't tell him about the tearful soon-to-be mom's phone call late last night.

"I miss my mom," Courtney had said. "She should be here. I can't do this without her." Kim had cried with her, and then prayed for her until the sobs quieted.

Lord, we don't always understand Your ways and

honestly at times like this, it is hard to accept them. We miss Aunt June. Please help Courtney lean back into Your comforting arms. Help her remember that You are her loving heavenly Father, and Your love can bring her a peace that is beyond our wildest dreams.

"Have you talked to her today?" Larry's voice brought Kim back to the present.

"Last night. I'm hoping to get up there next week to see her."

"Stop by on your way. I'll load up your car with some of the supplies. Maybe I'll be able to get to my bookshelf again."

"Will do," Kim said. "I've got to go. Your son is on the other line."

"Got to love that boy's timing," Larry said. "Try to bring him with you when you come by."

"Bye, Uncle Larry." Kim ended their call then answered Aaron's line. "Hello, dearest. Your dad sends his love."

17

You're My Favorite

Aaron had been back for several days and the normal office routine had returned. Inventory was over, and projections for the new fiscal year were made. Kim noticed that Aaron was keeping to himself again. Joyce noticed too.

Kim suspected he and Gigi were getting more serious. "That could be why he's avoiding me," Kim said to herself during a coffee break one morning. "He knows I wouldn't be able to keep my mouth shut."

"Talking to yourself again, my dear?" Joyce had come in the break room as Kim dumped the coffee she had just poured into the sink. It was no longer appetizing.

"Just mumbling about Aaron," Kim said and returned to her office. Her bad mood continued as she stared at her computer. The dance studio sent periodic reminders about their Friday night programs. It had been almost a month since the Friday night confrontation with Aaron at the restaurant. The memory of his actions in the hallway brought a blush to her cheeks. She shook the thoughts away and concentrated on the good that had come from that evening.

She and Mitchell had been on several casual dates since that evening, a fact Kim had kept from Aaron. Kim knew he would feel the need to interfere. Kim didn't want to send mixed signals to Mitchell, anyway. There was a graduate school intern at the office, and Kim had been trying to find a way to introduce Peggy to Mitch. But that was a task for later. She stared at the computer screen again.

Chip would be willing to go dancing, but Kim didn't want to face Aaron's teasing. Wishing she had someone else to invite, Kim mentally went through the Sunday School list. The only men she could think of either were already in a relationship or would consider her invitation an opening for one.

"Maybe I should just go hang out at the bar one night," she said to herself, not seeing Joyce in her doorway. Kim jumped at the sound of her voice.

"This habit of talking to yourself is disconcerting," Joyce said. "Surely, we're not that desperate, are we?"

"No," Kim said. "Besides, Aaron would have a cow if I did. I'm just missing the fun of dancing."

"Ask Aaron," Joyce suggested.

"Not sure Gigi would appreciate that." Kim was suddenly intent on cleaning up the files strewn across her desk. When Joyce didn't respond, Kim glanced up to see a somewhat guilty look. The older lady seemed to check herself, and then delivered her news.

"Well, never mind. Stanley is here with some new samples. Although, I'm sure you could tell he has arrived." Joyce pinched her nose. Kim laughed.

"Yes, I *sense* his presence now," Kim said. The two ladies hid their laughter as the box and container salesman came across the office in response to Joyce's summons. Stanley was known for his use—or overuse—of cologne.

"At least it's a new scent," Joyce whispered right before the slick salesman reached them.

Thirty minutes later Kim was incapacitated. She had reacted violently to Stanley's new fragrance. Delivering an Oscar worthy performance, Stanley never suspected that Kim was suffering from a blinding, nauseating headache within seconds of his stepping into her office.

After he left, Kim stumbled to the small bathroom in Aaron's office, afraid she was soon going to be sick. Aaron was having lunch with a business associate next door at Lucy's. Kim forced down a painkiller she had managed to grab from her drawer, hoping she could keep it down. Joyce had followed her into Aaron's office.

"What's wrong?" Joyce helped Kim settle onto the couch in the darkened office.

"Migraine." Kim curled up on the couch.

"Was it that gosh-awful scent Stanley was wearing?" Joyce asked as she settled Aaron's windbreaker over

Kim's form. Kim nodded then groaned as the slight motion increased the pain. "What can I do?" Joyce's voice was full of concern.

"Dark, ice, prayer," Kim managed to mumble. "And coffee?" Joyce jumped into action. A bag of ice in hand, Joyce thanked Peggy for the cup of coffee. The young office clerk had overheard Kim's request.

"Is there anything else I can do?" Joyce made sure the blinds were closed completely after she settled the ice pack on Kim's forehead.

"No, thank you, Joyce." Kim's voice was barely audible. "Aaron?"

"On his way," Joyce saw Kim's small smile peak out. "Peggy called him."

"Hey." A few minutes later, Aaron's quiet voice came through the fog of her pain. A gentle hand stroked her cheek and forehead. He was sitting on the coffee table next to the couch. Kim grasped his hand.

"Please just shoot me now."

"That bad, huh?" Aaron asked as he massaged her temple. "If you think you can walk, I'll take you home." Kim nodded slightly, squeezing his hand as even that small movement shot more pain through her head. Aaron swung her legs off the couch and sat her up slowly. The office was eerily quiet as he walked her out through the side door.

"We'll leave your car here." Aaron put her carefully into the passenger's seat. He reached across her, buckled the seatbelt, and leaned the seat back slightly. "We can get it tomorrow."

"If I survive." Kim leaned her head on his shoulder. Aaron draped his arm across her lap and rested his hand on her knee.

"You haven't had one of these in a while." The sentence was more of a statement than a question. Kim held up two fingers.

"Two months?" His brow furrowed. "How did I miss that?" Kim shook her head and winced again.

"Two years?" Kim gave him a weak 'thumbs up' not trusting her ability to survive even a simple nod. When they got to her apartment, she insisted on walking herself to her apartment, but allowed him to settle her in bed.

"Meds?" He asked as he opened the medicine cabinet in her bathroom.

"Green bottle," Kim said. Aaron found the headache relief pill and filled a cup with water.

"Will this be strong enough?" He sounded doubtful.

"Should be." Kim's voice was still weak. Aaron settled on the bed next to her, leaning against the headboard. She curled up close to him, her pillow against his side.

"Try to sleep." He rested his arm around her back, his hand on her waist. He lightly rubbed her neck and shoulders with his free hand.

"Okay." She closed her eyes but her brows were still furrowed. When he was sure she was asleep, Aaron leaned his own head back, eyes closed. Kim slept for half an hour and when she stirred, she reached for Aaron. He was gone. Pain shot through her head as she bolted upright. Her groans as she sank back onto the pillow brought Aaron back to her doorway.

"Hey, you," he said. "You didn't think I had abandoned you, did you?" Her tears answered his question. "Does it still hurt?" His calm voice gave her a chance to recover.

"Yes." She felt stronger now and sat up gingerly. "But I know I'll live. The pain is mainly in one spot now and I'm not nauseous any more."

"Do you want coffee? Some toast?" He asked. She smiled weakly, knowing that toast was about the extent of his culinary skills. He considered pre-packaged meals in a box to be marvels of the modern world.

"That sounds great," Kim said as she tentatively swung her legs off the bed and stood up. "I'm going to change clothes. If you hear a loud thump, you might want to come make sure I haven't succumbed to the dizziness." Aaron's eyes widened and she heard a choked cough.

"Aaron Graham Mercer, are you blushing?" Kim's teasing caused him to blush more.

"No." Aaron's protest was not very convincing, especially given his sudden bolt down the hallway. "Just be careful."

Kim joined him in the kitchen a few minutes later, now clad in baggy sweatpants and sweatshirt. These would service as pajamas later so she wouldn't have to change again. She didn't tell Aaron that most of the changing process had been carried out on the bathroom floor where a wave of dizziness had landed her.

"Smells delicious." She slid cautiously onto one of her swivel bar stools. "Quite a fancy spread you have here, mister."

"How's the pain? Better?" Aaron joined her, a plate of toast, two mugs of steaming coffee, butter, honey, and jelly set between them.

"Um-hmm." Kim licked her lips between bites. "I'm hungry, but a little leery, so this is perfect."

"Well, eat this and I can order some take out if you feel up to it." They decided instead on mac-n-cheese and a salad. She settled on the couch, leaned her arms on the end of the overstuffed back, and watched him read the directions on the box.

"Do you need my help?" She was enjoying this domestication of her best friend.

"I think I've got this, sweetheart," he said. "I do have a college degree, remember? Turn on the basketball game and leave me to my masterpiece."

While the noodles were cooking, Aaron pointed to a photo on Kim's bookshelf.

"Why didn't you tell me about Lamar's wedding?"

"What do you mean?"

"That you were in his wedding." Aaron moved back to the kitchen.

"I didn't know I needed to get your approval," Kim said. "Courtney knew. I thought she would have told you."

"Courtney doesn't tell me everything," Aaron said. "Obviously you don't either."

"Consider it payback."

"For what?" Aaron drained the pasta and studied the back of the box for the rest of the directions.

"You know," Kim said. "Not letting me talk to you about Gigi." Aaron turned toward her, spoon in mid-air.

Tell her about Gigi! What are you waiting for? Aaron's smarter self screamed inside his head.

"I don't want to fight with you tonight, Kim," he said instead, then forced some humor into the situation. "It would be unfair in your weakened condition."

"Meanie." She stuck out her tongue at him. "I should call in reinforcements. Courtney might take your side, but Amanda would be on mine." She couldn't resist adding fuel to her argument. "And Ben, of course."

"Now who's being mean?" Aaron set her meal in front of her on the coffee table. "Are you trying to make me jealous, too?"

"I'm too hungry and feeble for such a difficult task, my dear." She sighed as she settled back, the warm bowl in her lap. "This is yummy."

They ate the rest of their meal in silence, Aaron intent on the game and Kim still weak from her ordeal. She was an avid sports fan but sleepiness was winning tonight. During half time, Aaron cleaned up their dishes.

"You're very domestic this evening." Kim watched him from the couch, her folded arms perched on the back of the couch.

"I have many hidden talents you know nothing about." He tossed the dishtowel at her. It landed on her head.

"Nice shot." She settled back onto the couch. "Despite our earlier conversation, is it okay if I break the Rule and tell you that I hope Gigi appreciates how lucky she is? I was thinking how differently Scott, or any of my other former boyfriends, would have handled today. I can't imagine any of them taking care of me like you have."

"Why on earth would I ever let anyone else take care of you?" Aaron had turned to put the dishes away, so his quiet comment didn't reach Kim.

"Come back and watch the game." Kim patted the sofa cushion next to her. "Halftime's over."

"Feeling better?" Aaron asked as the third quarter ended. "Are you going to be okay after I leave?"

Kim gave him a thumbs up from her sprawled position. Her head was resting on the pillow he had propped next to him on the couch. His arm was draped along the back of the sofa, but he would occasionally rub her back or gently massage her neck. He switched to the weather station as the basketball game went to commercial.

"Aaron?" He turned the volume down.

"Yes, my dear?" He brushed the hair back from her face. She sighed.

"You're my favorite." He could see her closed eyes and slight smile.

"Your favorite what?" Aaron asked, teasing her now

that she was recovering. "Sports star? Boss? Friend? Super Hero?"

"No, silly." She poked his leg, but her voice let him know she was almost asleep.

"You're my favorite..." she paused, "...everything." Aaron's hand froze mid-air. He sat silently as her breathing slowed. When he slipped from under the pillow and grabbed his phone, Kim stirred. She settled right back to sleep, so she missed the words Aaron said when he called Geoff and Courtney.

"I'm in trouble."

18

Something Foolish

"What have you done now?" Geoff asked.

"Is Courtney there? Can you put her on the phone with you?" Aaron's voice concerned Geoff so he immediately put the phone on speaker mode.

"Aaron? What's going on? Is Kimberly okay?" Courtney asked. Aaron had asked Joyce to call Courtney and Geoff, because he knew they would worry when Kim didn't call for a baby update. After assuring them that Kim was indeed recovering from the migraine, he explained why he had called.

"I think I've done something very foolish." He took a deep breath.

"Are you going to tell us or do we have to guess?" Geoff asked when Aaron didn't continue.

"I've fallen in love with Kim," Aaron finally blurted out. Confiding in two of his closest friends, he expected sympathy, not laughter, and definitely not cheers

"Yes! I knew it!" Geoff said.

"Oh, Aaron, I'm so glad." Courtney's voice was full of emotion. "What did she say?"

"Say? Are you kidding? I haven't *told* her. This is crazy." Aaron was frantic.

"Not necessarily!" Courtney countered.

"Well? What should I do?" Aaron asked. "I'm a little desperate here. How can I face her at work everyday now? Should I fire her or resign myself? Ask my dad to transfer me back to the plant? Help!"

"Slow down, buddy!" Geoff said. "Let's go back over this and maybe you can see a way out."

"What if I don't want a way out?" Aaron muttered.

"Talk to us, Aaron," Courtney said. "We're not doubting you, but you'll have to give us some more information if you want to know what to do next."

Aaron described the transformation that had occurred over the last few weeks. As best he could tell, it started with the wedding. Enjoying Kim's company that evening—dancing with her, laughing with her, basically flirting with his best friend—was in sharp contrast to barely tolerating Gigi.

"Speaking of Gigi," Courtney said. "What are you going to do about her? Seems to me you haven't mentioned her in a couple of weeks."

"She broke up with me." Aaron could hear Courtney's

celebration.

"Does Kim know?" Geoff asked.

"No," Aaron said, "and I don't want her to hear it from anyone but me. I'll tell her when—and if—the time is right."

"I think you should tell her. Her reaction might be very informative." Courtney's comment earned a bitter laugh from Aaron.

"Oh, yes, I can hear it now. ' Kim, Gigi broke up with me, but that's good, because I've discovered I'm in love with you!'"

"Sounds good to me," Geoff said. "Concise and to the point. Perfect."

"Why did she break up with you?" Courtney shushed her husband. Aaron hesitated once again. He chose his words carefully.

"She told me that I was paying too much attention to Kim," Aaron said. He heard the Bentons sharing a laugh. "Hilarious, I know, but that's the reason I haven't told Kim about the breakup. She took the Savannah Rule a little too literally this time. I knew she wasn't thrilled with Gigi, but I was too stubborn to pick up on her subtle hints."

"You still haven't told us what specifically happened tonight that was the knock out punch," Geoff said.

"Great metaphor, Benton," Aaron said. "I feel like I've been punched. We were laughing at the thought of any of her former boyfriends, our friend Scott included, spending their evening taking care of her. They would be useless."

"Then? What happened?" Courtney asked.

"She said I was her favorite."

"That's it? We've been saying that to each other since high school!" Courtney said.

"Yes, but she added something this time." Aaron glanced back into the apartment to make sure Kimberly was still asleep on the couch. "She said I was her favorite *everything*."

"Oh, wow. Good luck, buddy." Geoff said. "We have to go now."

"Very funny," Aaron said. "I don't expect you two to fix this, but you've got to convince me not to do something stupid, like tell her."

"Even if you did tell her, I'm not sure she'd believe you, especially since you didn't tell her about breaking up with Gigi," Courtney said. "I think you're right, too, when you tell her about Gigi, she's going to guilty."

"Great. Tell her. Don't tell her. You guys are not helping." Aaron slumped against Kim's patio wall. "Maybe I'll just sleep on it and hope that it's just a bad case of indigestion."

"Sounds like a plan to me," Geoff said with a laugh.

"That is a good idea. Sleep on it, Aaron," Courtney said. "Make sure you're sure before you do anything drastic."

"Are you warning me off, Courtney?" Aaron asked. "You don't sound too confident. Do you think I'm making a mistake?"

"No," Courtney said, her laugh easing Aaron's tension, but only slightly. "I'm actually thrilled, even if I did lose the bet Geoff and I made at the wedding."

"So, Geoff, you knew, and didn't warn me?" Aaron asked. "Thanks a bunch!"

"Anytime, Aaron," Geoff said. "Courtney knows best, though, so I'd listen to her if I were you."

"Right now, all I can think about is some other guy here taking care of her and how much I'd like to drag him out by his collar." Aaron saw that Kim was stirring and quietly opened the patio door as he ended the call. "Courtney, do you think I have a chance?"

"Yes, dearest," Courtney said. "But she may take some convincing."

The Bentons, not knowing what other advice to give, promised to pray for Aaron.

Half an hour later, Aaron tucked Kim under her bedcovers.

"I'm going to live." She had whispered her okay for him to go. "I'll be able to sleep it off now. I'll see you in the morning."

"You sure?" Aaron said, sitting on the edge of her bed. *She has no idea how much I want to stay right here,* he thought. *I have no idea how I'm going to hide this from her.*

"Bring me a good cup of coffee," she said, as he got ready to leave. "I'll probably be starving, too."

***

Having slept so much of the evening away, Kim found herself wide-awake a little after midnight. She decided to get a shower so she could sleep later in the morning. Getting out of the shower, she was rudely reminded of her weakened state. Dizziness from the ordeal and lack of food caused the bathroom to spin. Clutching the towel hanging on the rack had not completely broken her fall, and she hit her head on the edge of the tub. A small cut and good-sized knot served as reminders of her foolishness.

She was still getting dressed when she heard the front door open the next morning.

"Hungry?" Aaron called down the hallway. She stuck her head out of her bedroom and waved. His eyes widened when he saw the bandage. He reached her in two strides.

"What did you do?"

She backed up under his charge. Her fluffy turquoise bathrobe covered her pinstriped slacks and camisole completely, but she still felt strangely exposed.

One arm around her waist, Aaron cradled the side of her head, tilting it so he could investigate her injury. She swatted his hands away and squirmed to be released. The half hour she had spent figuring out a way to hide the evidence on her forehead had been wasted. She had forgotten that it would be visible while she was blow-drying her still damp hair.

"I just forgot that I'm not Superwoman. Now go away so I can get dressed." She almost fell when he let go of her quickly. She clutched his jacket as he steadied her. Regaining her balance, she moved back to her dresser.

"You might want to wear a different suit jacket." He called down the hall as he retreated to the kitchen. "The lovely robe you're wearing doesn't match your slacks and might cause a stir at the office." She rolled her eyes, but grinned, knowing his comment meant he wasn't too upset about her injury.

"Don't roll your eyes at me, either," he said. She laughed at his psychic abilities. As she came around the counter a few minutes later, Aaron was holding out a cup of steaming coffee for her.

"Thank you for taking care of me." Before taking his offering, she wrapped her arms around his waist and rested her head on his chest.

"No problem." Aaron patted her back with his free hand, moved her slightly to his side, and retrieved his own mug. "You still seem a little wobbly."

"I'll be better when I get something on my stomach." She made no move to leave her current position, even though Aaron wasn't returning her embrace, and was now holding both coffee cups.

"Here's your coffee," he said. "Do you want to sit here in the kitchen or on the couch?"

Kimberly ignored him. "Do you think my boss would let me stay here today?"

"I hear he's a nice guy." Aaron put down the coffee mugs and ignored Courtney's voice in his head telling him to take it slow. He would take it slow tomorrow.

This morning he chose to enjoy the feel of Kim in his arms. "I'm sure he thinks it's an excellent idea for you to stay home today."

As she relaxed against him, he knew he was in danger. Warning bells sounded in his head and he captured her hand that was now moving up his chest.

"No, I don't mean stay home." She tapped his chest with her fingers that were trapped beneath his hand. "I mean stay *here.*"

"Don't be ridiculous." Aaron abruptly moved her out of his arms and reached for the mugs. "Find a seat and drink your coffee."

"Fine." Slightly dizzy from the quick movement, she plopped into a chair and watched as he removed the fresh cinnamon rolls from the oven. "You're no fun."

He refused to look at her, knowing she would be using her adorable pout to try to get her way. Her request had been made in jest, but Aaron knew he was in danger if he let her stay wrapped in his arms. Letting her think he was impatient with her was safer. He let her wield flattery from the sofa.

"These are delicious." She licked her fingers. "You are becoming quite the chef. You're going to make someone a wonderful husband one day."

"Eat." His clipped tone caused Kim to stare, the confusion etched on her face. Aaron handed her a napkin as she licked her fingers once more.

"Sorry," she said. "I know I'm a mess."

"I'm serous about you staying home today." He

refilled her mug and watched her eat another pastry, intent on each bite she took.

"After spending the night with me, I realize the thought of having to endure my presence for another eight hours is onerous." She stood a little too quickly and he grabbed her as she swayed.

"You have no idea." His cryptic response was barely audible as he steadied her. Realizing she was misinterpreting his aloofness, he stretched the truth to preserve her feelings. "I'm not trying to avoid you. Go get back in bed, or get ready to go." He gently turned her toward the bedroom. "Either way, I'm leaving in five minutes."

"Sir, yes, sir!" She saluted and went to brush her teeth. When she reappeared, he risked a glance over her, head to toe, and then turned to gather the suit coat he had thrown off when he arrived.

"Good choice," he said, pointing to her shoes. "Come here." He hadn't forgotten about the bruise and lifted her dark bangs to check it before they left. He brushed his fingers gently across the offending spot then traced one finger down her cheek.

"I'm not sure this is a good idea." He tilted her chin up and shook his head.

"I'll be fine," she said, then moved away. She grinned as she opened the door. "Plus, you'll be there to catch me if I fall again."

"Yes, I will." Aaron said as he locked her apartment door behind him. "Always."

19

Let's Do Lunch

With the approaching due date, Kim and Aaron took turns calling Courtney every day. Their first question was always the same.

"Baby yet?" Kim knew the answer, since Courtney had promised to call day or night at the first sign of labor, so she brought up her latest Aaron issue.

"Something's wrong with Aaron," Kim complained, "again. It's almost as if he's avoiding me but trying to make it seem like he's not. It's bizarre." Courtney's hesitation in responding concerned Kim. "Are you sure you're feeling okay? You're awfully quiet."

"I'm fine," Courtney assured her. "Aaron's probably worried about me. He's taking this Uncle Aaron role very seriously."

"True," Kim said. "He will be so disappointed if Baby Abigail doesn't love and adore him like every other woman in his life does."

"Every other woman?" Courtney's was quickly followed by Geoff's voice in the background.

"Wife," his voice warned. "Behave."

"What's up with Geoff?" Kim asked. "What are you not telling me? Or is the concern I hear just nervous Daddy syndrome?"

"Since he's more anxious about the whole process than I am, I'd say that's the issue," Courtney answered. "I'd better go. Love you. Give Aaron a kiss for me." Kim laughed as she heard Geoff's response in the background.

"Courtney Joy Benton! Behave!" Kim laughed, but wondered what was so mischievous about Courtney's words.

End of the month reports and files needed attention, so Kim called Aaron on the office intercom to let him know Courtney was still doing well. He had been in and out of the office for weeks, attending conferences and new product shows. Kim knew he was going to be disappointed if Courtney had the baby while he was out of town.

"She also said to give you a kiss," Kim added to her baby update, "but I'm swamped, so you'll have to come get it if you want it." She heard a crash and his muttered curse.

"No, I'll pass," he said. "I need to go. I just dropped my mug and made a mess."

"Sorry about that," Kim said. "I'll add it to your tab."

"My mug?" Aaron asked.

"No." She laughed at his confusion. "The kiss." When her comment was met with silence, she knew the Grumpy Aaron was back. "I'll let you go."

It had been a couple weeks since her migraine. Aaron was acting odd, but Kim had been preoccupied with training Peggy. Some days he seemed like the same comfortable best friend she used to enjoy, and others he was grouchy and distracted. She was glad when Old Aaron reappeared a couple days later.

"Let's do lunch," Aaron said as she brought him the weekly purchase order summary. He rarely checked them, so it didn't surprise her to see him put it in the 'to be filed' box without a glance.

"Hey there, mister." She folded her arms in mock annoyance. "I work hard on those reports! I expect you to read them front to back."

"I'll get right on that," he said, "after lunch."

"Or never," she said. "Where do you want to eat?" They chose a new pizza buffet down the street. As Aaron slid into the booth, his plate piled with a variety of pizza and pasta, Kim settled into her salad.

"Is there anything left on the buffet?" Kim asked.

"Funny." He placed two of the slices on an extra plate. "These are yours. The sausage pizza was almost gone and I knew you'd cry if you didn't get any."

"How sweet." The hint of sarcasm didn't detract from her appreciation. "Does this mean my old friend Aaron has returned?" She popped a piece of sausage into her mouth. "If so, I'm so relieved. Grumpy Aaron was a bore."

"I've been grumpy?" He busied himself with rearranging his substantial feast. "I hadn't realized it."

"Well, the rest of us did." She reached across and wiped marinara sauce off his chin. Aaron batted her hand away. "Maybe I spoke too soon." She dropped the napkin back on the table. Aaron changed the subject.

"Did you call Courtney today? It's your day, right?"

"No, I was going to wait until later. She had an appointment this morning. Maybe she'll have some news." Kim's phone beeped as she finished her sentence. She laughed. It was Courtney.

"Hey, girlie, you must be psychic," Kim said. "Aaron and I are eating a late lunch and we were just talking about you. I'm going to put you on speaker." The restaurant was almost empty since the lunch crowd had already cleared out. The back booth that they had chosen meant their conversation wouldn't disturb any of the few remaining diners.

"You're eating lunch with Aaron?" Courtney's voice registered her surprise.

"Why do you sound so surprised?" Kim asked. Aaron decided he needed a refill. "He's been a grouch lately, but seems to have recovered somewhat. I'll have to assume it's a Gigi thing, but he's invoked the Savannah rule, so I can't ask him about it. He knows that I like Miss Georgiana, but not necessarily as a future wife for him."

"Is he listening to you right now?" Courtney's

disbelief was almost palpable.

"Nope, went to get more soda," Kim said. "So, what did the doctor say? Oh, Aaron's back. Say hello, Aaron. Courtney seems to think I'm just pretending that you're here."

"Hello Courtney." Aaron responded obediently. "What did the doctor say?"

"I'm pregnant." Courtney's deadpan answer was typical of her dry humor. "Not sure how it happened." Unfortunately, Aaron had just taken a drink of his soda and was now choking.

"Hold on, Courtney," Kim said. "I may have to give Aaron mouth-to-mouth. Your last comment seems to have taken his breath away." Aaron waved her away frantically. "Never mind, he seems to be more afraid of the cure than of choking to death."

"Fine," Aaron sputtered. "I'm fine." Kim's grin earned her a warning wave of his fork.

"He's fine, but I may have to explain the birds and the bees to him," Kim said. Aaron dropped his fork. Kim raised an eyebrow. "He seems quite confused." Courtney was breathless with laughter. "Wow, you must really be pregnant," Kim continued. "You've never thought I was that funny before."

"Any estimate on Abigail's arrival?" Aaron finally turned the conversation back to its original topic after he recovered his composure. He frowned at Kim. "Behave," he mouthed.

"No signs yet," Courtney said. "Kim, you might have

to explain what I mean." The pair could hear her as she dissolved into giggles again. "But really, everything is looking good. Since I'm technically not due until next week, there's no reason to panic yet."

"Okay," Kim said. "We love you. Or at least I do. Aaron seems to have lost his voice again."

"Are you okay, Aaron?" Courtney asked. Aaron picked up the phone, turned off the speaker, and marched outside. Kim watched in helpless silence. *Something was definitely going on.*

"What was that all about?" Courtney asked when Aaron gave the all clear. "You don't seem to have made any progress."

"I suggested lunch because I can't think straight when I'm not around her." Aaron paced back and forth on the sidewalk in front of the restaurant. "But I can't think at all when I am."

"You're in love, my dear. I'm just glad Kim hasn't come right out and asked me what is going on with you. I don't think I could keep my big mouth shut."

"I haven't been home long enough to deal with it properly. I'll face it when I'm done with these trade shows."

"Coward," Courtney tempered her words with a laugh.

"True," Aaron said. "You're not helping much, though."

"Here's my advice," Courtney said. "Tell her about Gigi."

"No way." Aaron glanced through the window and saw that Kim was still picking at her food. "I can just imagine Kim's reaction. I'm not going to put her through that guilt trip."

"I think she would be thrilled that you guys broke up," Courtney said. "Besides, how would she know the real reason for the breakup unless you told her?"

"She would see right through any story I told her," Aaron replied. "The fact that Gigi figured out my feelings before I did really bugs me, too."

"Well, don't wait too long, dear." Courtney softened her voice.

"I'm not making any promises," Aaron said. "Don't have that baby until I get back."

"I promise. Give Kim my love, since you can't give her yours." He hung up to the sound of her laughter.

Kim tried unsuccessfully to ignore the awkward silence that fell over the table when Aaron returned.

"I won't ask you what's going on." She tried to keep the hurt out of her voice. "You would tell me if something is wrong with Courtney or the baby, wouldn't you?"

"They're fine, I promise," Aaron said. "I'm the one dealing with something and Courtney is sticking her cute little nose into it."

"Oh." Kim stood quickly. "I'm going to get some pie, do you want some?"

"Honestly, Kim, they are fine." Aaron grabbed her hand briefly. "I have something I need to work through, and I promise I'll explain when I'm ready." He waited until she nodded. "And, yes, I'll take a piece of pie."

"Have you talked to Scott recently?" Aaron asked as they ate their desserts. "Or Michael, Marshall, Marcus? What was his name?"

"Mitchell," Kim said. "No." Dishes clinked as she started staking their plates and cleaning up his considerable mess. His secret conversation with Courtney had stirred up frustrations Kim had thought she had buried. Their reappearance was annoying.

"Are you mad?" Aaron asked.

"Perhaps I need my own Savannah Rule. Which sounds better? The Scott Statute? Kim's Command?" she said. "Oh, I know. The Mitchell Mandate!"

"You're upset."

"Your powers of observation are uncanny. I'm not upset. Just tired of people who are in relationships being so concerned about my lack of one." The napkin she wadded and tossed on top of the dishes was an unspoken exclamation point. "I'm going to pay. I'll meet you at the car."

"Hold on there, missy." This time Aaron caught her by the strap of her purse. He pulled her around to face him as he stood. "I care about you. I have a right to be concerned." His grip on her bag tightened. His clipped words were drawing attention from a nearby table. "You deserve someone who not only loves you, adores you, and protects you," he said, "but someone who *likes* you as well."

"I agree wholeheartedly." Kim peeled his fingers off her purse. "God has decided I have to wait, apparently. As hard as that is for me to accept, I can't change it." Tears of humiliation were threatening. "Until the time when He brings someone to me, I will thank you to mind your own business!" She tugged free and headed to the cashier's desk.

As she paid, she saw Aaron slumped back in his seat, head buried in his hands. Two months ago, even two weeks ago, she would have headed back to his side. Today, she did not. The silent ride back to the office was broken only by her parting question.

"You'll be out of town again next week?

"Yes," Aaron said, and for the first time in years, let her open her own door. "Please tell Joyce I have an errand to run."

20

I Love You Like a Sister

"I can't wait for next week," Kim said under her breath as she stepped back into the office.

"Why is that my dear?" Joyce asked.

"Nothing." Kim quickly changed the subject. "Aaron's running an errand. Do I have any messages?"

"Yes," Joyce said. "My dear nephew called. I thought he was just confirming the numbers for the charity dinner dance, which he was, but he also wants you to call him back."

"Lovely," Kim said, her tone indicating otherwise. "Could you do me a favor and not tell Aaron that Scott called?"

"Unless he asks me directly," Joyce agreed, "I won't tell him." Her look expressed her concern. "Is anything wrong?"

"Not really," Kim said. "Just a little too much drama

at lunch. Thanks."

When Kim returned Scott's call an hour later, Aaron was still not back in the office.

"I'm going to pick you up for an early lunch tomorrow," Scott said. "I'm craving Lucy's, too, if that's okay. Plus, that will give us plenty of time to talk." Kim was smiling after she hung up, just as Aaron stepped into her doorway.

"Please tell me that wasn't a call to hire a hit man," he said, an apologetic grin on his face. "I'm sorry for ruining our lunch. Forgive me?"

"Yes." Kim crossed her arms as she faced him. "I forgive you, but I can't figure you out lately. One day you're all giggles and grins and I can't seem to get you out of my office, then some days you're all moody and pensive." Aaron's lack of protest told her that her concerns were not a product of her overactive imagination. "I feel like something is going on with you and it frightens me. Please, Aaron. If I need to apologize for anything, tell me. "

Aaron's stare offered no clues. As he let her request sink in, he shook his head, clearing whatever thoughts were battling inside.

"Yes," he finally spoke. "It is something big, but I haven't made a decision yet. When I do, I'll need to decide how to tell you, because I'm not sure how you're going to take it."

"Wonderful." Her shaky laugh was accompanied by nervous rearrangement of the piles on her desk. "Now

I'm terrified. Thanks so much."

"My pleasure." Kim's breath caught as she saw Aaron's grin. It was so reminiscent of the charming best friend she loved. Feeling like he was slipping away, the last few weeks had shaken her world.

"Who was on the phone?" He perched on the edge of her desk, after moving one of the stacks of files she had just placed there.

"Scott. He's taking me to lunch tomorrow." Kim watched as Aaron's face fell and he suddenly remembered he had work to do. She made a face behind his retreating back. Peggy caught the look as she waited patiently outside the cubicle.

"Men." The young blonde handed Kim some invoices.

"More like *man*," Kim replied. "He's the only one that knows how to punch my buttons."

The next day as Kim slid into her chair across from Scott, she was struck again with the difference between this gorgeous young attorney and their mutual friend, Mr. Aaron Mercer. Her contemplation registered on her face.

"Is there a problem?" Scott asked. "You look perplexed." Kim blushed, and was glad he couldn't read her thoughts.

"I'm hungry!" Kim said. "I didn't eat breakfast since you said we were doing an early lunch."

"I'm glad the timing worked for you. I thought it would let us miss most of the lunch crowd." They ordered and talked about the charity ball while they waited for their food.

"My sister and her boyfriend will round out our table," Scott said. Kim knew that Joyce and Aaron would also be there. "I appreciate you all being willing to go. It's for a great cause and the food is supposed to be excellent, too." The waitress brought their plates and Kim decided a direct attack was the best option.

"What's up?" Kim asked. "I know you didn't ask me to lunch just to talk about the benefit dinner. I hope it's not bad news. The last month with Aaron has left me a little fragile around the edges." When Scott didn't respond right away, Kim put down her fork.

"Really?" Her shoulders sagged. "What have I done now?"

"First tell me why you and Aaron are at odds." Scott handed her a fry from his plate.

"We're not really at odds. It's just been a strange few weeks." Kim gave her ex-boyfriend a quick summary of the weeks following the dance lessons, including the headache rescue and the bizarre lunch yesterday. Scott's hesitation made Kim push her plate away, the sandwich half-eaten.

"Well," he said. "You might be in for a similar conversation today."

"Let me have it," Kim said. "I'd rather be hit while I'm already down. It's less distance to fall."

"First, I want you to know that I've prayed long and hard about this." He picked up her fork and fed her a couple more bites of her open-faced roast beef sandwich. "You're going to need sustenance," he said in response to her raised eyebrows.

"Great," Kim said. "Can we get it over with quickly?"

"You know I love you like a sister." Scott continued eating his meal, but watched her intensely as she took in his words. "Although we both know we're not right for each other, I'm still disappointed our relationship didn't work out." Kim could only nod. She tried to hide the rising dread each sentence brought.

"Kim, my dear." Scott's deep sigh warned her of the importance of his next words. "I know you told me one of the reasons you struggle with long term relationships is that being raised in a military family meant you moved around a lot. Personally, I think not forming deep relationships may have been a defense mechanism, at least until you met Courtney and Aaron."

Kim sat quietly now, steeling herself for whatever Scott was getting ready to say.

"But there's something more going on when it comes to relationships with men." Scott launched his salvo. "I think you set your sights too high."

She was glad she had already swallowed the last of her meal, because otherwise she would now need the Heimlich maneuver. Scott continued when her coughing turned out to be non-life threatening.

"Too high?" Kim asked. "You think I should settle? Like look for the first guy that will have me?" Her voice rose an octave.

"No, no." Scott smiled. "Maybe 'too high' is the wrong term to use. ' Too specific' may be more accurate."

"You've totally lost me now." Kim thanked the waitress as the young lady refilled their drinks. The coughing fit had caught the teenager's attention. They ordered a slice of pound cake to share for dessert, along with some coffee. The lunch rush had still not begun and Scott was glad for the privacy. They fell silent as the steamy cups of coffee and delicious cake were delivered. Scott drank his coffee black, so he continued his discourse while Kim added creamer and sweetener to hers.

"My dear, describe your perfect man." Scott calmly took a large forkful of the chocolate baked goodness. Kim blinked in surprise at his sudden change in tactics.

"Excuse me?" Kim asked. "I'd rather just sit here and eat cake, if you don't mind." She took a big bite to emphasize her point.

"Tell me what you're looking for, and be as specific as you want." Scott folded his arms and waited.

"Okay," she conceded. "Tall, dark, handsome." Kim watched the swirls in her coffee mug as she stirred in more creamer.

"C'mon, Kim, this is serious." Scott's tone was still friendly, but she could sense that he was ready to switch to courtroom attorney mode if necessary. Kim had no desire to be cross-examined by the successful young lawyer.

"Fine!" Counting off her list on her fingers she began, "Loves God, loves me, wants children, good sense of humor, smart, has integrity, well-respected by his peers and co-workers, nice family, his friends like me." She took a breath and closed her eyes. "Tall, but not too tall, nice eyes, but the color doesn't matter." Her nose crinkled as she conjured up her preferences. "Likes sports, wouldn't mind traveling, likes dancing, but that we could negotiate." She opened one eye and saw Scott watching her intensely.

"Are you done?" he asked. She gave a small shrug.

"I guess so. I can't think of anything else, and some of those are not even deal-breakers."

"You're halfway to confirming my suspicions," Scott said. "Be patient. I'm going to ask you one more question that may seem odd. You need to answer it as best you can, but you may need to think about this one for a while. You may want to close your eyes again." Kim obeyed. "Describe your wedding to me."

"This is really weird," Kim said, peaking once again. "Did you learn this technique in law school, or are you a closet psychic?"

"C'mon, Kim," Scott said. "You're a smart girl. I know you can figure this out. Think."

"Okay, okay." She closed her eyes reluctantly. "Aaron's there, of course, but he's scowling now." She heard the jingle of the diner door behind her and opened one eye when she heard Scott laugh.

"Speak of the devil." Scott squeezed her hand. "Aaron just walked in. Therapy session will have to be suspended. Here he comes. Smile."

21
Privileged Information

"Are we having a psychic session here?" Aaron's words were thick with sarcasm making it clear he had observed Kim's closed eyes and hands clasped gently in Scott's.

"Mercer," Scott stood and greeted the subject of their supposed metaphysical session with an outstretched hand. "We were just talking about you." Kim kicked the back of Scott's leg under the table. Aaron hesitated but finally shook Scott's hand.

"We'd ask you to join us," Scott added, "but we're having an important conversation."

"That is obvious." Aaron's eyes were boring into Kim's. He turned back to Scott. "I'm sure I don't need to issue a new warning to you." At Kim's huff of protest, he raised one finger. She fell silent.

"I will choose to not be offended by your implication." Scott's tone held a warning of its own.

"Have a nice lunch then. Kim I'll see you back at the office in a timely manner, I'm sure." His brusque nod was dismissive as he went to pick up his order.

"Oh, he makes me so mad sometimes!" Kim said, stabbing the last piece of chocolate cake. She was tempted to throw it at Aaron, but instead fed it to Scott before scraping the last of the frosting up for herself.

"Let me know when he gets his food," Scott said. Kim tried to make her observation inconspicuous, as she glanced once more at the counter. She saw Aaron's scowl deepen and knew he had been watching them. A minute later, he left the diner.

"He's gone. I need to get back, too." She stacked the plates and silverware. A nervous habit didn't fool Scott.

"Nice try, sweetheart." Scott motioned for the check. "We need to finish our session. This is your last chance to tell me you honestly don't know what I'm trying to tell you."

"Not a clue." Kim smiled sweetly. "I was a little scared you wanted to get back together, but I know you're too intelligent for that. I'm nothing but trouble, you know."

"Right." Scott laced his fingers with hers and pulled her along with him to the cashier. "Plus, we're too much alike for the relationship to be healthy." He paid for their lunch and they walked out into the beautiful spring day. "I'm glad we walked. You have a few minutes before you need to be back, so we're going to enjoy the sunshine and I'm going to finish my lecture."

"Yes, counselor," Kim said. "But as my attorney, you know that anything I say is privileged information."

"True." Scott found a bench in the newly renovated urban park next to the diner. "Kim, since we broke up, I've spent a lot of time praying for you. Falling in love with you would have been the easiest way out of the mess, but I know we both realize that wasn't going to happen."

"Despite the fact that we are both irresistible, beautiful, talented, wonderful people." Kim leaned her head on his arm. "Oh, and modest, too." She sighed. "I do know that I'm the one to blame. I just can't figure out what my problem is."

"I know exactly what your problem is," Scott squeezed her hand. "You have a bar set that most men cannot reach."

"You said that my expectations are too high. What did you mean?" She didn't hide her frustration. "I want someone that will love me for who I am, but who will also encourage me to be better, kinder, and less judgmental. Someone who'll laugh with me and at me. Someone who looks forward to an evening out, but also savors the times we stay home with our kids in front of a roaring fire." Her words tumbled out.

"Is that all?" Scott hid a grin.

"No. I'd like someone to take me on explorations of new places, and go with me to visit old familiar ones. Someone comfortable and exciting all at the same time. Someone I can give my life to, making his life better."

By the time Kim finished, Scott was laughing.

"What is so funny?" Kim asked. "Am I asking too much?"

"No, your ideal is not too lofty." Scott stood and pulled her into a hug. "Like I said earlier, it's just too specific." She felt his deep sigh.

"Specific?" Kim asked. "I don't understand."

"You, my dear," Scott said as he lifted her chin, forcing her to meet his eyes, "just described your relationship with Aaron Mercer." Her silence stretched out as Scott watched the blood rush from her face, only to return in a blush across her cheeks. Kim pushed away from him.

"That's ridiculous!" She turned abruptly and headed quickly for the refuge of her workplace, forgetting that Aaron would be there.

"Wait, Kim!" Scott trotted after her. He caught up just outside the lobby door and pulled her back into his arms. "I know it's a shock but think about it. You measure all your boyfriends by some unspoken standard. The more I thought about it, the more it became clear. Aaron is who you picture waiting for you down the aisle."

"Because he's the best man, or a groomsman," she sputtered. "Or the flower girl!"

"Or the groom." Scott had not released her so she could feel his laughter. "I'm going to let you stew on this for awhile. Like I said, you're a smart girl. You'll see the truth eventually."

"Impossible." Kim shook her head against his chest.

"Even if I did believe you, what difference would it make?"

Scott pulled out of their embrace. "Look at me," he said, to be sure she was listening.

"Kim, you need to consider the possibility that you're in love with your best friend." Scott kissed her gently on the cheek and let her go.

22

Consider the Possibility

Somehow, Kim made it across the office without having to speak to anyone. As she watched Scott return to his car from her window, he gestured for her to call him. She nodded then slumped down in her chair.

A knock at her door made her jump. She blinked the tears away and took a shaky breath. Aaron opened the door without waiting for permission. Kim watched as his expression went from annoyance to concern and then settled on anger.

"What did he do?" Aaron came around the desk and knelt by her chair.

"Nothing." Kim batted his hands away. "I'm fine. Please just leave me alone." She spun her chair away and grabbed the stack of files behind her desk.

"Kim, talk to me."

"Please, Aaron, I need to get back to work," she said. "Leave Scott out of this." She heard him hesitate at the doorway.

When she turned back around, he was gone. Aaron avoided Kim the rest of the day.

The next morning, Joyce handed Kim a note when she arrived. Aaron was leaving a day early for his conference in New York. Kim relaxed. She had until Tuesday to make some major decisions.

She had spent the first hours of last evening mentally mocking Scott's suggestion. *Ridiculous idea. Me, in love with Aaron? Impossible.*

Several hours later, still wide-awake, she had to concede Scott was closer to the truth than she wanted to admit. She would need several days to work through the idea of being in love with her best friend. She prayed for guidance.

Lord, what is going on? Scott's idea is bizarre, but I'm frightened that he's right. Please help me deal with the doubts that he sparked. I need to trust that You will guide me through this emotional maze.

***

Early the next morning, Kim stared at her reflection in the office bathroom mirror. "How could you let this happen?"

"What did you let happen, my dear?" Joyce's voice startled Kim. Kim sometimes thought that the older lady could read minds. She hoped this wasn't one of those times.

"Oh, nothing," Kim said. "So, Aaron flew out early?"

"He did," Joyce said. "Seemed like a last-minute decision, but I guess that's why we always buy the flexible tickets." Kim kept her face as expressionless as possible and escaped to her office.

Peggy spent the first part of the day helping Kim sort out the inventory results. The distraction of teaching the young worker the nuances of the accounting procedures helped Kim get through the morning. She had a growing confidence in Peggy's ability and after lunch, this confidence led to a drastic decision.

Kim closed her door and cleared off her low filing cabinet. As she sat staring out the window, Scott's words kept drumming through her head. She had made a list of the pros and cons of confessing her feelings, should she choose to admit them, to Aaron. The list habit, as Aaron called it, was hard to break. Kim glanced at her trashcan. Several wads of paper were evidence of her lack of success. *I need help.*

Asking Courtney for help was out of the question. Not trusting herself, Kim kept her daily call to the expectant mom shorter than normal. Tempting as it was, there was no way she was going to put her very pregnant best friend in the middle of this mess. Sometimes whispers of teenage insecurity resurfaced and Kim was afraid that, if faced with having to choose between the two of them, Courtney would pick Aaron. So, falling back on every child's first line of defense, Kim called her mom.

"Is the baby here?" Kim's mom was anxiously awaiting news of Abigail's arrival, just as they all were.

"No, mom," Kim said. "I talked to Courtney this morning and the doctor still says it could be any day now, or it could be two weeks."

"So, as delighted as I am to hear from you, why the call today? You're very predictable and we didn't expect to hear from you until the weekend—except with baby news, of course." Kim called every Sunday afternoon and whenever she needed advice from her handy-man father.

"I'm in trouble." Kim knew her statement would surprise her mom.

"What's wrong, dear?" Elaine Calhoun knew her daughter rarely admitted vulnerability, and she could hear the distress in her voice. Kim decided to get the painful admission over with quickly. Blaming it on Scott was an easy choice, too.

"Scott has charged me with something and I need confirmation that he's crazy," Kim said. "I'd like to make him an appointment with a psychiatrist." Her parents had met Scott when they visited Kim before Christmas and had trusted Aaron explicitly when he assured them that Scott was a man of integrity. They also knew that Scott had broken up with Kimberly several weeks ago.

"I take it you two are still talking to each other," Mrs. Calhoun said, "and you haven't lost your sense of humor, so tell me what terrible deed he has accused you of committing."

"Are you sitting down?" Kim asked. She needed her

parent to agree that the ludicrous idea Scott had proposed was indeed absurd.

"Well, now you have my curiosity peaked," her mom said. "I'm sorry your dad's not here. He went to pick up the missionary family from the airport. Did you remember they'll be staying here while we're out of town the next couple of weeks?"

"Yes, I remembered. You can tell him later. I'm sure you'll both get a good laugh." Kim took a deep breath. "So basically, Scott thinks I've set Aaron up as some ideal and I measure every other man against him. That's why I can't stay in a relationship very long. Isn't that ridiculous?"

Kim's straightforward declaration was met with silence.

"Mom? Are you there? Are you okay?"

"I'm here and I'm fine, but more importantly, are *you* okay? If the idea is so ridiculous why has your announcement upset you so much?"

"It wasn't my announcement," Kim protested. "It's Scott's crazy idea."

"Are you sure it's crazy?" Her mom's calm voice annoyed Kim.

"Really? I called for support, not to have you join Scott's side," Kim said.

"I am not taking sides, Kimberly. I simply think you need to consider the possibilities. There must be something Scott has observed to make him come to that conclusion."

"I can see you're going to be no help at all," Kim said. "Thanks so much. Should I call later to talk to Dad? Maybe he'll be more sympathetic."

"He'll agree with me, sweetie," Elaine said. "I think Scott may be right. Are you sure that's all there was to his conversation? Your frustration seems a little out of proportion if Scott simply suggested you view Aaron as some sort of ideal. I don't see that as so out of the question."

"So now I'm overreacting?" Knowing any denial would be completely transparent, she hoped her mom wouldn't press her for more information. Kim resisted verbalizing Scott's closing argument, knowing now that he was probably correct. She decided to ignore her mom's last statement. "Isn't it enough to think that I'm so close-minded about men that I've put my best friend on some sort of pedestal? No wonder he's so secretive about his love life."

"What do you mean?"

"Nothing," Kim mumbled. "What am I supposed to do now?"

"Are you admitting it may be true then?" Elaine asked. "If you think about it honestly, it does make sense."

"It's nice to be abandoned so easily." Kim didn't hide her disappointment. "You're taking Scott's side."

"I am not abandoning you and neither will your father. There's no reason to takes sides. We all love Aaron and having a man of his character as an ideal is not a bad thing. Understanding that may be helpful. Just don't get ahead of yourself. Have you talked to Courtney about this? Seems to me she would have a helpful and unique perspective."

"I'm not going to ask her to step into the middle of this. Not right now," Kim said. "She has enough to worry about, remember?" She fell silent.

"What can we do to help?" her mom asked. Kim had expected shock or surprise, not the composed reasoning she was getting now.

"I haven't decided," Kim said. Knowing she was being childish, Kim apologized to her mom. "Sorry to be such a baby about this. Thanks for listening to my ranting."

"Thanks okay, sweetheart. That's why I'm here," Elaine said. "Do you want me to have your dad call when he gets back from the airport?"

"No, I'll be okay. Just talking about it has helped," Kim said. Resolve was forming in her mind, but she didn't want her parents to worry, or think that she was panicking. "I'm thinking about taking some time off. Not that I'm agreeing with you, or with Scott, but I do think I need to get away for awhile."

"That might be a good idea," her mom said. "Your dad and I can swing by there on our way out of town if you need us to."

"No, you guys will be busy getting your guests settled and getting ready to go. I think I may be making a bigger deal of this than I need to." Kim hoped her ploy to downplay her anxiety worked. She didn't want her parents to worry, and especially didn't want them to feel like they needed to check on her constantly.

"You'll still be in contact with Courtney every day, won't you? I wish we were going to be here, but we can't back out of our plans this late."

"Thanks, Mom," Kim said, a catch in her voice. "Could you do me one last favor? Please don't tell Aaron or his parents."

"We won't," Elaine said.

23

An Escape Plan

"I've got to get out of here," Kim said when she called Scott later. She was perched once again in her office window, watching the rain. It was a perfect match for her mood. "Thank you for not gloating."

"I wish you sounded happier," he said. "I don't think you should make such a radical move. Why can't you see that telling Aaron might be a good idea?"

"And ruin any particle of friendship we still have?" Kim traced a raindrop running down her window. "No thank you."

"You're going to run away?" Scott asked. "How is that going to help? Either you need to tell him, or stay here, face your feelings, and get over him."

"I'm sure Gigi would be thrilled with the news," Kim said. "I can hear it now, 'Really, Gigi, I'm in love with your boyfriend, but it won't change anything. You all just go right ahead with your lives.' That would go over so well."

"Where will you go? And for how long?" Scott let her sarcasm slide. The fact that she was no longer denying the truth of his observation was a victory he hadn't expected to come so easily.

"It'll be better if you don't know," Kim said. "That way you won't have to lie to anyone who asks. I'll call and let you know I'm okay."

"How long are you planning to hide?" Scott's tone made it clear that he didn't think this was a good idea. "You *will* be at the charity dinner, right?"

"Yes, I promised you I would," she said. "Maybe Aaron will back out, but even if not, I'll live through one evening, I'm sure."

"Well, keep me in your prayers next week," Scott said. "When Aaron finds you've disappeared, he is not going to be happy."

"More like relieved," Kim muttered. "With the mood he's been in for the last couple of weeks, my being gone will probably help."

Kim spent the weekend composing her letter to Aaron. Hiding her plans from Courtney and Geoff had been torture but Kim didn't want to put their friend in the middle of the situation, especially with Baby Abigail due any day. Since Aaron was out of town, keeping tabs on the birth had fallen exclusively to Kim. Every time she called, she came close to telling one of them about Scott's take on her relationship with Aaron. Knowing it would upset Courtney was the only thing that stopped her.

"You sound tired," Courtney had said during Saturday's call. "Everything okay?"

"Shouldn't I be asking you that?" Kim deflected her friend's question. "What did the doctor say yesterday afternoon?"

"The same thing he's said for two weeks, 'Any day now,'" Courtney said. "I'm tired of waiting, but with Aaron out of town, I hope she waits until next week. I hope Mr. Mercer appreciates how miserable I am. You'll need to make sure he knows how inconvenient his globetrotting is."

"I'm sure he'd rather be at the hospital visiting a lovely newborn girl," Kim said. She missed him, now even more as she was coming to grips with her feelings. Sadness crept into her voice.

"Are you sure you're okay?" Courtney pressed again.

"Yup." Kim forced a laugh. "Just a little tired. With Aaron gone, I have to take up the slack here. How thoughtful of him, right? I'll call you tomorrow after church."

Monday morning Kim showed up to work early, needing the extra few minutes to gather her courage. She stopped in Aaron's office first, knowing that if she didn't do the deed early, she might change her mind. As she moved a stack of files to put her letter right in the middle of his desk, she saw a receipt. The logo on the top of the slip caught her eye. It was from a small family-owned jewelry store. The owners were members of their church.

Kim couldn't help herself. She picked up the receipt. As the importance of what she saw sank in, the room spun.

24

The Receipt

Aaron's mood could only be described as elated. Done with the rounds of conferences and product shows, he would be home for several uninterrupted months. *Now to deal with Kimberly.*

Since his initial confession to Courtney and Geoff, Aaron had kept his struggles to himself. He knew it wasn't fair to put Courtney in the position of having to take sides. Joyce was the only other person that knew he and Gigi were no longer together, but even she didn't know about the purchase he had made last week. Seeing Scott and Kim together at Lucy's had forced Aaron to act.

"Kimberly knows something is going on with you," Joyce told Aaron before he left on his last trip. "I'm not going to push you for answers, Aaron, but I'm here if you need to talk. I think I know what you are struggling with, but will limit my advice to this: you're going to have to come clean soon."

"Not until I'm sure there's a chance," Aaron had said, his words confirming Joyce's suspicions. The box in his desk, had she known about it, would be evidence enough of his hopes.

As he walked into the office this morning, he pointed to Kimberly's office, his eyes questioning. Joyce shook her head. Aaron's brow furrowed as he looked at his watch.

Joyce poured his morning cup of coffee and gathered the day's files. She stopped suddenly at the doorway of his office. Aaron was staring at a letter in his hands.

"She's gone," he said. Joyce came to the desk and he handed her the letter. Kimberly had penned a concise but ambiguous explanation of her request for a sudden leave of absence.

"I know she's been moping around the last week," Joyce said. "Maybe something happened that caused her to need the time away."

"What have I done?" Aaron stared at the letter.

"What do you mean?" Joyce realized something major had happened between the two of them. Any hope she had of uncovering the mystery was unlikely as she watched him close down emotionally.

Joyce spent the rest of the day alternating between trying to distract Aaron and encouraging him to call Kimberly. Catching up on work that had been neglected while he was gone occupied most of their time, but she did manage to get him to call and leave a message on Kim's phone. Of course, Joyce would have been disappointed had she known the content of his message.

I'm back. Trip went well. Lots of new products to discuss with my Purchasing Manager. Unfortunately, she has run away. If you see her, please have her call.

***

The next few days everyone in the office walked and spoke softly. Their usually easy-going boss had returned from his latest road trip transformed into the Big Bad Wolf. Poor Peggy bore the brunt of his ire when he discovered she was in daily contact with Kimberly. One afternoon when he realized she had just spoken to Kim, he stormed to the door of Kim's office where Peggy was creating the month's reports.

"Next time she stoops to call us, please tell Her Highness that we need some new letterhead." His curt words to the nervous young lady reached Joyce's desk.

"Aaron Mercer!" Joyce's voice cut across the office. Aaron hung his head.

"Sorry, Peggy," he said. "Blame it on jet lag." He bestowed one of his charming smiles on the young lady. Peggy's eyes were wide in surprise at his lightning quick attitude change. She nodded. Aaron left work early, to the relief of the rest of the staff.

"He's really mad," Peggy told Kim the next afternoon. "He seems to know exactly when you call. I think he's

147

just worried. I wish you'd let me tell him where you are."

"No!" Kimberly said. "Please, Peggy. You're the only one there who knows. I hate to put you in this situation, but I can't talk to him right now. He'll understand eventually." After she went over the necessary updates, she was impressed with how easily the young woman had conquered the nuances of the job. When they were done, Kim asked to be transferred to Joyce.

"Joyce, this is Kim. Please don't let Aaron know I'm on the phone."

"Yes, I understand," Joyce said, turning away from Aaron's line of sight. "How can I help you?"

"I'm fine, Joyce," Kim said. "I know Aaron is furious, but I can't face him right now. I'm not going to tell you where I am, because I don't want you to have to lie to him, okay?"

"Yes, that will be fine." Joyce continued the subterfuge, trying to make it sound like she was on the phone with a client. "If you're sure there's nothing else you need, I can do that."

"You're a dear," Kim said. "Keep you-know-who away from Peggy. She's terrified. I'll see you at the ball, okay?"

"Thank you for calling." When Joyce hung up, she looked over her shoulder. Aaron was standing in his doorway, arms folded.

"Was that Kim?" he asked. Joyce nodded. Aaron stayed behind his closed door for the rest of the afternoon.

25

Keeping Secrets

Peggy was sitting at Joyce's desk, giving Aaron's assistant a chance to grab lunch. The young lady's eyes widened as a tall stranger stepped into the office.

"Is Kimberly Calhoun here?" Mitchell Harper asked. "I was hoping to take her to lunch, but she's not answering her phone."

"No, she's not here." Peggy pulled out the message pad. "Can I give her a message?"

"Are you Peggy Giles?" Mitchell's smile caused Peggy to blush. "I'm Mitchell Harper." Kim had blatantly played matchmaker and told Mitchell all about her attractive and available co-worker. Although Mitchell and Kim had enjoyed their casual dates, he knew that she was not interested in a romantic relationship right now.

"Yes." Peggy recovered some of her composure enough to shake his outstretched hand. "She's mentioned you. I'm sorry she's not here. I can give her a message when she calls this afternoon."

"May I ask where she is? I've tried to reach her for a couple of days, so I'm a little worried. Is she okay?"

"Yes. I can't tell you where she is but I promise she is fine. She took some personal time." Peggy's smile reassured Mitchell. The affect his presence was having on the young woman meant that she didn't hear Aaron's door open.

"Mr. Harper. It's nice to see you." Aaron's voice startled Peggy, who recognized that his tone meant that her boss was not pleased at all to see Mitchell. The men's handshake did nothing to thaw the chill. "If you're looking for Kim, she's not here."

"Miss Giles has just informed me. Although I'm still concerned that I haven't been able to reach her, I'll take this young lady at her word and trust that Kim is well."

The young lady glanced from one man to the other, ready to referee if necessary.

"How's the job situation?" Aaron's abrupt change of topic didn't seem to confuse Mitchell.

"Very good, thank you," he said. "Looks like I'll have to get used to being called Detective Harper."

"Congratulations." Aaron's good wishes were sincere, but were tempered with his next question. "Does that mean we'll be seeing more of you around here?"

"Perhaps." Mitchell's glance directed at Peggy caused the young lady to blush. Aaron saw the interplay and relaxed.

"Well, it was good to see you again," Aaron said. "I'm sure Peggy will deliver any message to Kim."

"She won't talk to him," Peggy explained to Mitchell when Aaron returned to his office. "He's not very happy."

"That I could tell," Mitchell said. "So, I know Kim would be thrilled if you would go to lunch with me in her place." Kim had tried several times to arrange an introduction between the two, but the one time Mitchell had picked Kim up for lunch, Peggy had been out of the office on an errand.

"As soon as Joyce returns," Peggy said, "I'd be delighted to, Detective Harper!"

***

That evening, two hours north of the city, Kim sought assurance from Aaron's dad.

"No, we haven't told him you're here," Aaron's dad informed Kim as she placed the newly organized dishes back into the cabinet. "He's dropped hints about your mysterious disappearance, but we honored your request, no matter how much we disagree with it. I think he would be more upset about you working at the plant than he would be about you taking over his bedroom."

When Kim had called two weeks ago, asking for a place to stay, Aaron's parents had been concerned, but agreed to keep her secret.

"I'm so sorry to have put you in this situation." Kim hung her head to hide her blush. "I just didn't know where else to go. My parents are frustrated that they couldn't let me stay there, but the missionary family was in dire need while they are here on furlough."

"I know we promised not to press you about what happened between you and Aaron," Mrs. Mercer said, as she handed Kim another stack of plates, "but we'd like to help if we can." Aaron's parents had realized both young people were miserable. And stubborn.

"It's more my problem than his," Kim said. "I want to get out of the rut I've dug for myself. I need a new start. Aaron, I'm sure, wants to get on with his life, too."

"Please try not to bear this burden on your own," Gina said. "You have talked it out with someone, haven't you? Courtney? Your mom? Someone?"

"I've talked a little to my mom, but until I'm sure about what I need to do, and why, I don't want to dump all my problems on anyone else," Kim said. "Especially Courtney." The older couple watched her nervous movements. Kim tended to use house cleaning as therapy. The Mercers house had been transformed into a spotless model over the last two weeks. "Scott Delaney knows, and although he doesn't agree with my methods, he has been helpful. I'm sure he's hoping I'll get over my pity party soon, though."

Kim appreciated the leeway both her parents and Aaron's were giving her. She only wished she could tell them about her suspicions, but Aaron would have to be the one to share his plans to propose to Gigi with his parents. As for her parents, her dad had stated his opinion clearly, and then didn't bring the matter up again.

"We love you and I can promise that we are praying for you," her father told her when he had called to check on her. "Whatever has happened between you and Aaron needs to be fixed, but I can't, and won't, force you to deal with it. You're a grown woman and are responsible for your own choices, as much as we may disagree with them."

"Thanks Dad," Kim said. "I think." She knew she had her parent's love no matter what, but Kim was still battling the reality of her change in feelings for Aaron. Part of her wanted her deep, but platonic, friendship back, but she knew that loving him would be almost impossible to give up.

Working on cataloging the plant's annual inventory while waiting patiently for the baby's arrival, was a welcome distraction. Kim had also secretly contacted one of their suppliers about an opening at their new location. The new branch was three hours away from the Atlanta office and even further from her parents and Courtney. Although it would be hard being that far away from her parents and the new baby, Kim knew this was a great opportunity, for both her career and her sanity.

When the company called to set up an interview, Kim was thrilled. She had been staring at the calendar, knowing the charity dance was rapidly approaching. Scott's disappointment was the only thing keeping her from backing out. At least now she'd have something to occupy her mind on the eve of the event.

26

Do You Want to Hold Her?

The call from Geoff came around two in the morning. Kim was in the car and on her way to the hospital within minutes. Aaron's parents had heard the call and let Kim know they would be there as soon as they could after church. Larry had deacon duties during the service, and Gina figured it would give the young couple time to settle in before being inundated with visitors

When Kimberly had called last weekend, Gina knew immediately that something major was wrong. Over the next few days, she realized the situation between their son and his best friend was strained, but didn't push either of them to explain what had happened. She was curious but smart enough to give them time to figure it out on their own.

"Are you still planning to stay with them when they come home from the hospital?" Kim asked. "I know Geoff's mom isn't coming until next week."

"Yes, but it'd be fine if you want to stay with them the first couple of nights." Aaron's mom had confided to her husband that she hoped Courtney and Geoff would be able to get Kimberly to open up about Aaron.

"That would be nice." Kim grabbed an overnight bag. "I'll call you as soon as we have any news." She gave her adopted aunt a hug. "This is exciting, isn't it?"

Twelve hours later, Kim was holding the precious package while Baby Abigail's parents whispered quietly.

"He's on his way. I warned him that she was here." Geoff brushed the hair away from his wife's tired face and kissed her forehead. His wife giggled. The effects of the mild pain medication she had begged for during the delivery were wearing off, but she was still slightly giddy.

"Maybe we should warn her instead," Courtney said. "I hate that he won't let us tell her and he won't tell her so we can't tell her." Her jumbled words were slightly slurred.

"Hush, sweetheart." Geoff placed his fingers over the new mom's lips. "You'll get us both in trouble. Even though you may not agree, we promised him. If we don't let them work this out themselves, you'll never know if you pushed them into something that wasn't meant to be."

Kim heard them whispering and sent them a confused look. Geoff just smiled, just as his phone beeped. *Perfect timing,* Geoff thought as he looked at the message from Aaron.

"Aaron's on his way up," Geoff said. Kim ignored the announcement. She was standing at the window, still cradling the baby. The baby's bright blue eyes were showing signs of drowsiness. Kim knew that she would have to hand Abigail over to Aaron when he arrived and dreaded the interchange. Being in the same room with him was going to be torture enough, let alone having to transfer a sleepy baby into his arms.

She could see the door's reflection in the window, so she knew exactly when he arrived. A petty sense of accomplishment made her smile as she watched Aaron try to ignore her presence. He went immediately to Courtney's side and gave her a warm, brotherly hug. Kim tried not to laugh at his awkward attempt at gentleness.

"Do you want to hold her?" Geoff asked him. Aaron's jaw dropped.

"Excuse me?" Aaron choked out. Geoff laughed.

"The baby," Geoff said under his breath.

"Oh," Aaron said. Kim watched them from under lowered lashes, wondering what Geoff thought was so hilarious. As Aaron made his way around the bed, Kim tensed.

"What did you do to your hair?" Aaron reached to grab the shortened locks, but let his hand drop as she leaned away from him.

Kim had taken the idea of starting over quite literally. She shopped for new clothes and visited a fancy salon for a new hairstyle. It wasn't a drastic change, but the long dark hair that used to hang halfway to her waist had been shortened to wavy curls that fell just below her shoulders. The new style framed her face and made her hazel green eyes stand out.

"Hush, baby." Kim rocked Abigail gently. Aaron's harsh tone had startled the newborn. "Uncle Aaron's bark is worse than his bite." Kim's comforting tones calmed the baby immediately. "I'm going to let him hold you if he promises to behave." Her raised eyebrow warned him. She nodded to the recliner and Aaron settled himself in it.

"Sorry, Princess." Aaron's words were meant for Abigail, but Kim's heart wrenched. She placed the precious bundle in his arms, then boldly met Aaron's glare.

"My hair style is none of your concern, Mr. Mercer, and I will thank you to keep your opinion to yourself in the future." Kim quickly moved away from his stifling presence. She offered to get Geoff some coffee and check on Courtney's meal.

When she left, Aaron stared at the baby in his arms. Geoff came around the bed and took up the position by the window that Kim had vacated.

"When I saw her with the baby, I almost lost it," Aaron said, without looking up from the bundle in his arms.

"I'll bet," Geoff said. Aaron had called early Monday morning, when Kim had disappeared. He had downplayed how upset he was, mainly to protect Courtney from worrying. Courtney had reached out to

Kimberly when Aaron couldn't get her to answer his calls, but her attempts were met with firm resistance. Kim refused to explain why she needed time away from Aaron.

"Have you figured out what she's been up to for the last week?" Geoff asked. "Why didn't you just show up at her parents' house and make her talk to you?" Aaron shook his head, but didn't answer. He stared again at the baby whose tiny fingers were wrapped around one of his.

"She is magical," Aaron said.

"Abigail," Geoff asked, "or Kim?" He dodged the kick Aaron aimed at him. "You haven't decided to tell her yet have you?"

"Of course not," Aaron said. "Joyce said Kim had noticed the change in my attitude. Apparently, that change was unwelcome. As soon as she got wind of my misguided feelings, she bolted."

Thankful his wife had fallen asleep, Geoff merely nodded. If Courtney had been awake, he was sure she would have numerous suggestions for Aaron's next move. Geoff was adamant that Courtney, a helpless romantic, stay out of it.

With the warm drink in hand, Kim leaned on the wall outside of the hospital room and tried to catch her breath. Willing herself ready to face Aaron again, she pushed away from the wall and squared her shoulders. As she handed the cup to Geoff, her pounding heart was the only evidence of her discomfort.

"Aunt Gina and Uncle Larry will be here in a little bit,

so I'm going to scoot on out, okay?" Kim leaned over and spoke quietly to Courtney who had roused from her short nap. Kim didn't want to risk being in the same room with both Aaron and his parents.

Everyone assumed she was staying at her childhood home, but she was confident that the Mercers wouldn't reveal the truth about her temporary residence. Kim's real concern was that they would be able to read her anguish if they saw her with Aaron. So far, she had only told them that she needed a fresh start. The fact that she was in love with their son remained a secret.

Moving to Aaron's side, Kim took a deep breath. He looked so relaxed, holding the baby casually but carefully with one arm. As she leaned over the baby and kissed the downy head, her hair brushed across the back of his hand. She heard what sounded like a growl and saw his free hand clench the arm of the recliner.

"I thought you left." He pulled away from her as far as he could. Knowing her closeness caused him pain gave her no pleasure. Hiding her true feelings was her primary goal, so she decided going on the offensive would be her best defense.

"I'm sorry my presence is so oppressive." She kept her head down and blinked away the sudden tears. Their tense conversation caused the baby to stir in her sleep. Feeling the need to defend him once again to his newest family member, Kim leaned over and kissed the baby once more.

"Sweet Abigail, Uncle Aaron is not angry with you,"

Kim said. "His arrows are meant only for me."

"Kim." Aaron reached for her, but she had already moved away.

"Geoff, I'll call you before I head back here tonight, to make sure I bring everything you need." Kim hugged Courtney one last time and then was gone.

27

The Apology

Aaron stared at the doorway.

"Here." Geoff held out his phone. "I know she won't answer if she sees your number, but she'll answer if she sees mine. Give me my daughter and go fix the mess you just made."

Aaron kissed the baby gently before handing her over to her father. In the waiting room down the hall, he paced the floor for several minutes. Stopping at the window, he realized that he could see the parking lot below. He watched as Kimberly walked between the rows toward her car. *Better get this over with.*

"Did you think of something else I need to bring back? Let me pull out my list," Kim said as she unlocked her car door.

"It's me, not Geoff," Aaron said.

"What do you want?"

Kim slammed her door without getting in, staring at the phone. Aaron smiled. *At least she's not pretending to be immune.*

"I need to apologize." He leaned his forehead against the window, enjoying the chance to watch her without her knowledge.

"Go ahead. I'm waiting," Kim said as she leaned against her car.

"You're right. You can do what you want with your hair." He held his breath as he saw her run her fingers through the soft waves of the new style.

"Thank you so much for your permission."

"C'mon, Kim," Aaron said. "I'm trying here. The last week has been rough. You disappear, with no explanation. You won't talk to me, and now you're acting like it's my fault. What do you expect from me? I'm not Superman."

"At least we agree on something," she muttered.

"Kimberly Nicole." Aaron's voice was a growl. "You are the most frustrating, infuriating woman I know. Tell me why you left. Please."

"I did tell you," Kim said. "I needed to readjust my priorities. I've fallen into a boring routine, and wanted to shake things up a little."

"A little? You blow off your job, go into hiding, and pretend that it's no big deal."

"I didn't blow off my job." Kim slid into the driver's seat of her car. Aaron could no longer see her face as she continued defending her actions. "I'm in contact with

Peggy every day. She's doing a marvelous job. I know I didn't give a lot of notice, but I did have unused vacation days."

"Not a lot of notice?" Aaron asked. "Is that what you call leaving a note after the fact? If any other employee had tried this stunt, these two weeks would have been their last." *She has to know she's pushing my buttons.*

"What a tempting thought," she said.

"Don't push me," Aaron warned. He turned his back to the window. "Would you like me to make it official?" *You're an idiot! Stop, before it's too late.* Aaron ignored the warning in his head.

"Are you firing me?" Kim's voice rose slightly.

"If that's what you want." As his comment was met with silence, Aaron saw his parents weaving their way through the cars towards Kim. He heard her drop the phone.

Kimberly had been startled as Aaron's dad tapped on the passenger side window. She fumbled for the phone and waved at Larry and Gina.

"Your parents are here," she said. "Unfortunately, we will have to see each other next Saturday night, but be assured, that will be the last time you have to endure my presence. I'll come in early that next Monday and clear out my office."

"Kim." Aaron rubbed the back of his neck. "Kim?" He looked at the phone. She had hung up.

***

Aaron had barely greeted his parents at the hospital, pleading the need to make the two-hour trip back home in time to take care of some work issues. His hasty departure also prevented the interrogation he knew they would try to administer.

Geoff called him later that night. Kim hadn't hidden her distress well when she returned to the hospital with a change of clothes for the new dad and a contraband candy bar for Courtney. The honorary member of the trio was determined to discover what had happened.

"Spill it, big guy," Geoff said. "Courtney and the baby are asleep, Kim is back at the house, and you're going to tell me what you did to mess this up even further."

"I fired her."

"You what?" Geoff's shout turned the heads of the other late-night diners. He was glad he was downstairs getting a snack instead of in his wife's room.

"Fired her," Aaron repeated. "I think."

"Aaron, I know this will come as no surprise, but you my friend, are an idiot." Geoff's words were tempered by his sympathetic tone. "Tell me what you said, what she said, and I'll do my best to get you out of the pit you've dug for yourself."

Aaron went back over everything that had happened since the night of Kim's migraine. The truth about the jewelry store receipt was the only thing Aaron held back.

"Scott is still expecting you both at the ball this Saturday, isn't he?" Geoff asked as they wrapped up their conversation. "We'll be praying that you both get some clarity before then."

"Thanks, Geoff," Aaron said. "I haven't handled this well, I've put you and Courtney in a tough position, and managed to alienate my best friend—who happens to also be the woman I love. What a mess."

"I know you don't believe me," Geoff said, "but the best thing to do is tell her how you feel. She's not immune to you. Why not step out in faith and see what happens? Rejection would at least relieve the not knowing."

"True," Aaron said, "but it could take away any hope I have, too. I'm not ready for that. Kiss Abigail for me."

"I will." Geoff rejoined his wife and new daughter, his heart heavy for his friends.

28

The Seer

The picture was precious. Kim had snapped a quick shot when Ben wasn't looking. Engrossed with his new niece, Aaron's brother's blond head was bent over the bundle in his arms. He and Amanda had inherited their mother's lighter hair, while Aaron's darker shade matched Uncle Larry's. Abigail's blue eyes blinked as the young man waved a bright red teddy bear in front of her.

"You'll have to beat the girls off when I post this photo," Kim said. "Of course, they'll have to compete with Abigail. She seems quite smitten."

Ben stayed focused on the baby, but Kim saw him roll his blue eyes, so like his brother's. He was a fun and outgoing but was oblivious to how attractive he was. Kim remembered him as a young teenager, unaware of the girls vying for his attention. Aaron, almost seven years older, teased him about it until their mom stepped in.

Gina Mercer explained to Aaron that Ben idolized him and pointed out that Aaron's carelessness could mean he would miss out on a lifelong friendship with his brother. Aaron now called Ben at least once a week, checking up on his brother's studies, and keeping him accountable for his choices in the tempting environment of college life. Courtney had been Aaron's conscious during his college years and he knew her constant presence had made keeping his values intact easier.

"You'd better watch out, Kim. I may take one of them up on their offer." Ben grinned at her. "Then what would you do?" Kim and Ben had a running joke between them, threatening the rest of the family that they were going to run away together.

"Curl up and cry, my dear." Kim hugged him warmly from behind and kissed him on the cheek. "Unless, of course, she is kind, caring, and loves you more than you deserve. Then, I'd help her plan the wedding!"

"Whose wedding are we planning?" Amanda Mercer asked from the kitchen doorway.

"Ben's," Kim said as she helped Aaron and Ben's sister with the tray of drinks and sandwiches. Courtney had taken the opportunity their visit afforded to grab a quick shower and had warned them that she would be famished when she returned.

"So, Kim," the younger woman said as she stole the baby from her brother. "What's this about you quitting your job?"

"Is that what he told you?" Kim wasn't sure how much Aaron had told his family.

"I think there's more to this than either of you are telling me." Amanda's family had nicknamed her "The Seer" when she was in elementary school. She had an uncanny ability to read situations, but had learned the hard way to develop some tact in making her revelations. Aaron told the story of a nine-year-old Amanda revealing their great Uncle Denny's secret crush on the widow next door. The declaration was made quite publicly during a family reunion. The young girl didn't understand how not everyone could see the obvious puppy-dog eyes Denny made whenever the woman walked into the room. Gina had to teach Amanda when to keep her observations to herself.

"Oh great Seer, what do you know?" Ben teased his sister. "Kim obviously finally came to her senses and is getting as far away from Aaron as possible." Kim ate her sandwich in silence. Ben's observations were too close to the truth.

"Whatever," Amanda said. "Wherever you go, you'd better be back for my graduation, Kim. Where have you been the last week, anyway? What are you going to do?"

Kim choked on her last potato chip and was thankful her coughing meant she didn't have to answer right away. At least she knew Uncle Larry and Aunt Gina had kept her location secret. Aaron's siblings had come only to visit the baby and wouldn't be stopping by their parent's house.

"Right now, I'm weighing my options," Kim said. "I didn't officially resign, despite what your brother may have told you. He was the one who fired me."

"Aaron fired you? What an idiot!" Ben jumped to Kim's defense, playfully punching an imaginary opponent. "I can beat him up, if you like." Although Aaron was an above average athlete, even he would acknowledge Ben's superiority in most sport-related activities.

"Who are you beating up, dear?" Courtney joined them. She twirled around to display her outfit, a clean pair of baggy sweat pants, and one of Geoff's old sweatshirts. "Isn't my outfit adorable?"

Courtney was the most fashion conscious of the whole group, rivaling Gigi Peterson in her attention to style. Seeing her in such casual attire was unusual. Ben, always the most genuinely charming one stood and helped her to her seat.

"You look lovely, cousin," he said. "Nothing could detract from your beauty. You are glowing."

As the new mom enjoyed her lunch, she caught up on Ben and Amanda's recent activities. Amanda, still holding the baby, was observing Kim closely when she wasn't answering Courtney's inquiries.

"Abigail said she misses you." Amanda handed the baby back to Ben when she saw Kim start stacking the empty plates. "Keep Courtney company while Kim and I clean up."

"Spill it, missy," Amanda said as she took the stack of

dishes from Kim.

"I have no idea what you're talking about." Kim kept her back toward the observant young lady and filled the sink with soapy water.

"What did my brother do?" Amanda saw Kim's shoulders sink. "Why have my parents, or Geoff and Courtney, not stepped in?"

"They've been a little distracted, in case you haven't noticed." Kim busied herself with the dishes.

"Tell me, Kim," Amanda said. "I can be trusted. I know you haven't told Courtney the whole story. You still think she'll take Aaron's side over yours. I'm pretty sure she knows Aaron's side of the issue, though."

"What makes you think there are sides to be taken? Why can't everyone just believe that I needed to make a change? Besides, Aaron has made his feelings clear and I'm not going to fight him this time."

"What did he do, Kim?" Despite their difference in age, Amanda had always been one of Kim's confidants. She was also correct in her assessment that Kim was hesitant about confiding in Courtney whenever she had an issue with Aaron. It was the one imperfection in the trio's friendship.

"He started acting weird several weeks ago," Kim said.

"Weirder than normal?" Aaron's sister asked. When Kim only smiled, Amanda realized things were more complicated than she originally thought. "It's that bad, huh?" Kim nodded.

"I think he's going to propose to Gigi." Kim wiped her hands on a dishtowel. As she turned to face Aaron's sister, she saw the shock on Amanda's face.

"He wouldn't!"

"Yes, I think he would," Kim said. "I couldn't stay and watch him do it. If he's told Courtney, I would think she would protest, so I'm not as sure as you are that he's talked to her. I'm certainly not going to tell her. She doesn't need the worry."

Kim couldn't bring herself to tell Amanda the most painful parts. Aaron had stopped ending their conversations with "Love you," weeks ago. She also didn't mention the receipt, somehow hoping that not verbalizing it would mean there was a chance it wasn't true. Amanda was leaning against the kitchen island, arms folded, watching Kim intently.

"He doesn't know, does he?" she asked.

"Know what?" Kim matched her stance, arming herself as Amanda's expression made her nervous. She braced herself for the coming revelation. Hiding anything from The Seer was nearly impossible.

"That you're in love with him?"

Kim's silent tears were her only answer. Amanda hugged her and sighed.

"What a mess."

Kim left a half hour later, promising to make Amanda and Ben's excuses to their parents. Courtney was upstairs settling the baby down for another nap.

Amanda plopped on the sofa next to her brother.

"What's gotten you into a huff?" Ben asked as he finished off a second sandwich.

"Our idiot brother," she said.

"What did Aaron do this time?" Courtney asked from the doorway. The new mom eyed her cousin Amanda. *How much does she know?*

"Oh, the usual," Amanda said. "Ruining the best thing that's ever happened to him."

"Meaning?" Courtney busied herself picking up the remains of their lunch. She kept her question as neutral as she could. Aaron, and Geoff for that matter, would not be happy if she pried into whatever Kim shared with Amanda. *But if Amanda tells me on her own, I haven't done anything wrong, right?*

Amanda grabbed a handful of chips from Ben's plate and stuffed them in her mouth. "He and Kim are in a bit of a pickle." She smiled when Ben offered the dill spear from his plate.

"What has he done?" Courtney asked, knowing she was treading on thin ice, hoping Aaron would forgive her if she could get some information that would help his cause.

"He's doing something that will ruin their friendship forever. She's having a hard time accepting it."

"I know you don't want to betray her confidence, but are you sure that if he does whatever it is, she'll be upset?"

"Upset?" Amanda asked. "No, but devastated? Yes." Courtney's heart sank.

29

Here the Whole Time

Aaron pulled into his childhood neighborhood. Tomorrow night was going to be a battle, so he had decided to retrieve his best coat of armor. The last time he had worn his classic tuxedo had been at the formal Christmas dinner for singles put on by his parents' church. They had offered to have it dry-cleaned, so he had left it at their house.

At the top of the street, he recognized her car. For the first time in his life, he knew what the term "seeing red" meant. *They've known all along where she was. They hid it from me even though they knew I was in agony.* Aaron's fury was directed toward his parents. He conveniently disregarded the fact that he had hidden vital information from them also.

Kimberly heard the front door slam. She paled. Roxie's yips let her know exactly who was now bounding up the stairs. The Mercer's dog had been the family's Christmas present when Aaron was seventeen. The collie had gravitated toward Aaron immediately and was still his adoring worshiper. *It's too bad Roxie didn't think he was an intruder*, Kim thought.

The blow dryer dropped from her hand as she turned to wait for the coming confrontation. The furious man stopped at the bedroom door. Aaron's eyes raked her form, taking in the tattered robe and damp hair. He stepped slowly into the bedroom. The bedroom that was his and had been since he was a child. His fury was evident.

"Do you know the torture I've been through in the last two weeks? You were here the whole time?" Kim looked around her for a means of escape, eyes wide as he got closer.

"My parents are away and they had already promised a missionary family the use of the house." Her words tumbled out as she backed up. "I was at Courtney's for several days, until your parents were able to take my place. I'm going back home tonight."

"They were in on it?" Aaron pointed down the hall to his parents' room. "They could have told me last weekend at the hospital, but I guess it's good to know whose side they're on." He had followed her as she retreated. She stumbled on the pair of shoes she had carelessly abandoned earlier. He reached to steady her and, in the process, almost lost his balance. Six weeks ago, teetering in the midst of an embrace would've garnered giggles and fodder for months of inside jokes. Today, it bought panic. Kim grabbed for him as she started to fall, he instinctively pulled her towards him.

They froze for a moment, inches apart, eyes locked. Kim was not prepared for his reaction—or hers. She caught her breath as Aaron leaned closer. Roxie's bark broke the spell just before their lips met. Off-balance again as he released her abruptly, she landed on the bed. Silence filled the room as Aaron retrieved his tuxedo from the closet.

"I apologize for interrupting your morning." Aaron's voice was stoic as he took his time at the closet door, not turning to face her. "I didn't expect anyone to be home at this time."

Kimberly shook herself out of the shock of their embrace and tried to match his nonchalance. The shame that had washed over her now turned to anger. A fleeting thought that she may have seen a look of tenderness was quickly dismissed. If he wanted to pretend it hadn't happened, she was eager to oblige.

"I have an interview this afternoon." Kim's quiet words turned his head and garnered a raised eyebrow and furrowed brow.

"For a job?" His ridiculous question made her laugh nervously.

"No, for the Presidency." Sarcasm rose to her defense. She boldly met his glare. "Yes, for a job. For a company that's expanding. The new office is in Raleigh. If I get it, I'll start in a couple of weeks. The timing is right, since I'm in need of a new position."

"Fine." Aaron moved to the doorway. "Good luck."

"Thank you." Their stilted conversation was degrading rapidly. His deep sigh filled the quiet of his childhood bedroom.

"If you would prefer, I can tell Scott I won't make it tomorrow night." Aaron was hoping she would agree to his suggestion. He didn't want to face her again.

"No, I would hate for our..." she hesitated, "...*situation* to affect the evening. I can act like an adult if you can."

"Very well." Aaron nodded, his eyes meeting hers one last time. "Until tomorrow night, then."

It took all her fortitude to finish getting ready for her appointment. She was returning to her apartment this evening, too, which meant she had the chore of loading up her car with the belongings she had brought in two weeks ago. Knowing that she'd be cleaning out her office in two days, too, depressed her even more.

I'll deal with this later, she thought. *Or not.* Denial seemed a better choice. Unfortunately, the half hour trip to the interview gave her plenty of time to relive the confrontation.

The embrace was nothing like what she had dreamed. Foolish, romantic fantasies. Had they almost kissed? Doubts stormed through her thoughts. *It will be easier to pretend it didn't happen if I'll admit I imagined it.* Her flawed reasoning was little comfort, especially when she remembered his response. There was no doubt that the embrace meant little to Aaron. She hoped he hadn't sensed her vulnerability. How shocked he would've been to know how easily he could have taken their embrace further. Shame and self-doubt washed over her again. She prayed for peace.

Lord, please help me! I know now that I need to work my way out of his life so that we can both move forward. Please give me a peace through this interview. I know it is a perfect opportunity to let Aaron go. Help me to be willing to let that happen.

"Pull yourself together, Kim," she muttered as she entered the parking garage. In the elevator, she remembered that she needed to turn off her phone. As she pulled it out of her purse, she saw that she had missed a message. From Aaron. With a deep breath, she turned off the phone. She would decide later to read it or delete it. For now, she needed to concentrate on the interview.

An hour later, Kimberly was bidding the friendly administrative assistant goodbye. The interview had gone well. The company's expansion to the upstate area was encouraging and Aaron's dad had given Kimberly a glowing, if reluctant, recommendation. As promised, Aaron's parents had stayed out of the wake of whatever was going on between their son and Kimberly.

Alone once more in her car, she stared at the phone. Deciding that knowing was better than not knowing, she opened Aaron's message.

Please forgive my behavior. It was ungentlemanly and I hope you can someday forget it ever happened.

The emotional rollercoaster ended with a tearful two-hour drive back to her apartment.

30
Off to Battle

Dread. That was the only word Aaron could think of to describe the anticipation of this evening. Standing in Kim's office added to his misery. He picked up the picture she had left on her file cabinet. Taken during Christmas break their senior year in college, it embodied the trio's friendship. Flanked by the girls, he was standing under a sprig of mistletoe. The easy affection was represented so well by the kisses on each cheek. Flashes of Kimberly, in a worn bathrobe, in his bedroom, in his arms, did nothing to help his mood.

When he had decided to stop by the office, it was for one specific task, but he was having second thoughts. He replaced the picture and forced himself to complete his task. In his own office, he stared at the small box in his top drawer. Knowing now that it held an unwanted treasure, he slipped it into his tuxedo pocket along with the receipt. He would give them both to Joyce tonight and ask her to return it before she came to work on Monday.

As he glanced once more at Kim's office, Aaron thought of his conversations over the last two weeks with Courtney and Geoff. Their advice had been boringly consistent. His second cousin was filled with more romantic notions than normal and wanted him to tell Kimberly how he felt. Geoff was more reasonable, and encouraged him to try to get Kim to talk to him.

"I've tried." Just this morning, Aaron had told them after his encounter in the bedroom with Kimberly. Ashamed of his behavior, he kept the details of his latest blunder to himself. "She's going to take that job in Raleigh, anyway. She can't seem to get away from me fast enough."

"Isn't that a reason to take action now?" Geoff had insisted. "I can't believe you're just going to let her walk away without coming clean."

"I haven't told you guys everything." Faced with the prospect of the charity dinner dance being his last chance, he confessed the rest to the Bentons. "I bought a ring."

"What? That's great!" Geoff said. "So, you *are* going to do something. Finally!"

"No," Aaron said. "Kim saw the receipt. That's why she left."

"Wow, buddy," Geoff said. "That's big."

"Yes. How foolish was that? I'm pretty sure she saw

the receipt while I was on one of my trips." Aaron relived the plans he had made after Scott and Kim's lunch date had forced him to make a choice. "She left the next Monday."

"Are you sure?" Courtney finally spoke up. "Something was definitely going on in that brilliant brain when she was here. Did you talk to Amanda? They two of them seemed to be having a deep conversation the day she and Ben visited."

Aaron thought about the cryptic message he had gotten from his sister, and the unusual one Ben had sent.

I love you, but You Are an Idiot! Amanda had written in her usual straightforward fashion.

Wake up, goofus. Ben's had said.

"I don't know anymore," Aaron sighed. "Tonight's going to be torture."

"Call if you need to," Geoff said. "We'll be here."

***

The woman in a scarlet dress was a stranger. Her soft hair was swept up in a simple bun, secured with a jeweled clip. The dress was the one that had been purchased on a whim during the dance lessons. It was perfect for ballroom dancing, but now Kimberly was not so sure it was perfect for the charity dinner. The spaghetti straps left her shoulders and arms essentially bare, and the short, sequined inner layer ended several inches above her knee. The overlay was sheer and shimmery, flaring out to allow for easier dancing, but left her legs practically bare. Glancing at the clock, she knew she didn't have time to change. With a gold and scarlet wrap settled around her shoulders, Kim grabbed her small clutch and high heeled gold sandals.

Off to battle! She thought. *I only wish I had a suit of armor to face Aaron the Dragon.*

Valet parking was offered at the fancy hotel. As Kimberly pulled up, two young men vied for the chance to open her door. She smiled warmly at the pair.

"It's going to take me a little while," she said, swinging her legs out of the car. "I have to change shoes." The decision to wear flats to drive across town was easy. She hadn't thought about the likelihood of causing a stir while putting on the tricky heels. Negotiating the skirt of the dress in the confined area of her driver's seat added to the difficulty.

"Is there a problem here?" Kimberly cringed at the sound of Aaron's voice.

"No, I'm fine." She smiled falsely up at him. "Just changing shoes."

"Let me help, Cinderella." Aaron grabbed the sandal and knelt down. She shivered as he made short work of strapping one shoe on, and then held out his hand for the other. "Are you cold, Your Highness?"

"No. I could've managed fine on my own," Kimberly complained. She hated the spectacle they were creating.

"Ah, but these nice young men don't have all night to wait on you," Aaron said. "Plus, I'm sure they didn't pay extra for the show." Aaron's eyes were pointedly on her bodice. As she leaned over to fight over her shoes, she was displaying more than she intended. She sat back quickly and tried to pull her foot away. Aaron's grip was firm. Kim could feel every spot that his hands touched her calf. He finished the second shoe, and then helped her from the car. Keeping a grip on her arm, he reached in for her wrap and purse.

"Is this all?" He gazed back into her car.

"What else would there be?" Kimberly's irritation was evident in her voice, even as she turned a dazzling smile on the wide-eyed valets.

"I thought perhaps the rest of your dress was in the back seat. You seem to be missing quite a lot of it." Kim gasped. As Aaron walked her towards the elegant doorway, she could hear the chuckles from the car attendants.

"I'm sorry my appearance offends you." Her embarrassment gave her unusual boldness. Kimberly pulled her arm out of his grip. Knowing this was the last night she would see him for the unforeseen future, she decided raw emotion was no longer dangerous. At least letting him see her anger was better than letting him know how desperately in love with him she was.

As she stormed away, Aaron's arm dropped to his side. She saw his reflection in the mirrored walls of the hallway, raking a hand through his hair. He took his time before he followed her rapidly retreating form.

"Here comes Aaron." Scott told his aunt and nodded toward the side door. Aaron had bypassed the crowd at the ballroom's main entrance. Joyce was helping Scott rearrange the name cards at the table to insure less tension. She glanced up as her boss made his way across the room.

"My, oh, my." Scott's awed comment drew Joyce's attention to the stunning vision now approaching their table from the opposite direction. "Mystery solved."

"What mystery?" Joyce asked.

"I was wondering why Aaron looked so furious," Scott said as Kim reached the table.

"You are exquisite, my dear." Joyce greeted Kim warmly. "That dress turned heads all the way across the room. You will not want for dance partners tonight, for sure."

"Did you run into Aaron already?" Scott asked. Kim nodded, glancing back at Aaron who was watching them intensely. His now all-too-common scowl was back as he slowed his approach. "Looks like he's deciding whether or not to stay."

"My luck is not that good," Kimberly said, as she held out both hands to Scott. He pulled her close and she rested her hands on his lapels. Pulling him down for a kiss, she asked, "You don't mind, do you?"

"Not at all." He kissed her gently. "I'm glad 'If looks could kill,' is only a saying." She grinned. Tonight the offer Scott had made when they ended their relationship had the added benefit of irking Aaron.

Never able to mask his emotions, Aaron's mood was dark as he finally reached their table. Thankfully, Scott's sister and her fiancé Murphy arrived at the same time. Annette was gushing over Kim's dress as the men shook hands and located their seats. The adjustments Joyce had made meant Scott was flanked by his aunt and Kimberly. Aaron was relegated to the seat between his assistant and Scott's sister, leaving the handsome Murphy to share in Kimberly's attention.

The separation between the two combatants allowed for a relatively peaceful meal. Only once did Aaron's facade fall.

"Do we need to give those two some privacy?" Only Joyce heard his muttered complaint directed at the intimate conversation between Scott and Kimberly.

"Don't be crude." Joyce said as she patted his clenched hand.

31

A Calm Interrogation

Tonight's event was raising money for an educational initiative that provided opportunities for underprivileged children in third world countries. The organizers hoped to bring in close to a million dollars, mainly through the friendly competition between tables. Businesses across the city had sponsored tables for a set fee and the attendees could contribute additional funds. The winning table would receive a discount on the silent auction of artwork and antiques happening in the adjacent ballroom.

Between the salad and entree, some of the partygoers perused the auction selections. Kim and Scott chose to join the small group heading to the room where the available items were on display. As they made their way around the large room, he apologized for the awkwardness of the evening.

"I didn't think it would be this uncomfortable

tonight," he said. "My guess is that you still disagree with my solution for the problem."

"Yes, counselor," she said. "You are correct. I don't think telling Aaron how I feel will help me in any way. The choice to live in complete denial is my best option."

"Ah, yes, and you're doing it so well." Scott teased her gently. "No one would ever know that you two are at odds." Her ladylike sniff made her feelings clear.

"We're at odds?" Aaron's voice startled both Kim and Scott. The young attorney covered his surprise better than Kim did. His steadying hand stopped her from knocking over an expensive antique vase.

"Aaron." Scott kept his arm on Kim's waist until she recovered. "I was simply making an observation that I'm sure you won't deny. You and Kim are not enjoying the easy camaraderie that you have long treasured. I'll leave you two to talk." As Scott left to return to the dining room, Kim folded her arms and turned her back on her long-time friend.

"Kim," Aaron said. "He's right. We do need to talk." A slight shrug of her shoulders didn't convince him to leave.

"Did you get my text yesterday?" Aaron moved around the table so he could see Kim's face. "Do you forgive me?"

She glanced up briefly and nodded.

"Would you like me to leave?" He took a step closer to her.

"You made your feelings about having to spend the

evening in my presence clear in the parking lot." Kim pretended to be engrossed in the delicate pieces of pottery on the adjacent table. "What you chose to do is no concern of mine."

"That's nonsense and you know it." His soft touch as he turned her toward him sent tremors up her arm.

"My behavior yesterday was atrocious and I can only hope you can someday forgive me," he said. "My only excuse is that when I saw your car in my parent's driveway, I lost it. Since our encounter at the hospital, I've had no idea where you were, if you were okay, or what was going on. I handled it badly."

"I said that I forgive you," Kim said, without trying to free her arm from his touch. "We can act like it never happened." His gentle touch tonight, even as he railed at her while fastening her shoes, caused a flood of memories She had a fleeting wish for a time machine that could take her back three weeks. The easy affection they used to share was gone.

"I didn't say that." He continued his calm interrogation. "What have you been doing this whole time? Besides hiding in my bedroom?" Kim felt the heat move across her face and knew she was as red as the scarlet highlights in her dress.

"Working at the plant." Kim moved away from him hoping to cool her face down. "Your parents reluctantly agreed to keep my secret. As I said in my letter, I needed to think. Getting away from the everyday habits I had fallen into was the only way I knew to get the clarity I wanted."

"And? Did it work?" Aaron stepped in front of her, blocking any escape. He pulled her shawl up around her shoulders as he saw her shiver.

"Not really." Kim smiled faintly. "Moving away will help, though. I'm hoping to get good news about the job in Raleigh on Monday."

"You're actually going to leave me, just like that?" Aaron's control was slipping.

"I think we both know it's for the best." Kim set the delicate piece of china she had been examining back on the table. "Besides, you fired me, remember?"

"You know that was said in the heat of battle." Aaron didn't stop her as she moved slightly away from him.

"I'm tired, Aaron. The roller coaster ride of the last few weeks has been exhausting. Before I left, I was confused. One day you were like the old friend I've always known, the next you were railing at me." She watched his shoulders slump. As he started to respond, she held up her hand.

"I know I shouldn't have run away," she admitted, "but I did. I can't change that now. I had good reasons, but they don't really matter now." The emotions were starting to overcome her battle for self-control. She needed to get back to the safety of the others. "Like I said, I'm exhausted trying to handle the drama – both mine and yours."

Aaron watched her return to the dining hall. Her rambling words had done nothing to lighten his mood.

32

Last Dance

Aaron's attitude didn't manage to dampen the table's enjoyment of the rest of the dinner. Kim had chosen the salmon entree, a treat that she rarely took the time to make for herself. All the men had ordered the steak plates and received the teasing from the females with good-natured humor. The keynote speech began as the diners were finishing their entrée. The Congressman described the push to provide educational opportunities in needy villages across the globe.

"We will tally the tables' contributions and announce the winners later, but meanwhile our evening will continue with an open dance floor," the lawmaker said. "Dessert will be offered buffet-style later. Enjoy the rest of your night!"

"My lady." Scott stood and bowed over Kim's hand. "May I have this dance?"

"Certainly, Mr. Delaney." Kim stood and shook out the folds of her skirt. The sounds of a waltz were beginning to come from the dance band. Scott nodded to Aaron as he led Kim toward the wide dance floor. Aaron glowered.

"You do understand that I expect you to dance with him at some point this evening, right?" Scott asked Kim as they moved through the beginning steps of the waltz. "I need to be sure I got my money's worth."

"I think I'm coming down with a headache." Kim rubbed her temples. "Looks like this might be my one and only dance tonight."

"Coward," Scott said. "As your attorney I must insist that you stay engaged in your own case. No use trying to avoid the inevitable."

"Ah, but I can always claim insanity." Kim saw that Aaron was watching them intensely, so she smiled even wider.

"The Big Bad Wolf is watching us, isn't he?"

"Yup," she responded. "His mood swings are exhausting. I miss my fun-loving, easy-going, best friend."

"Be honest, though, Kim. You couldn't go back to your old relationship with Aaron now that you've admitted you're in love with him."

"I did no such thing!" Kim tapped Scott's cheek as the distinguished young lawyer rolled his eyes.

Aaron came out of his seat. Scott saw the movement and leaned closer, his lips brushing Kim's ear.

"I recall a certain waltz at a certain wedding between you and a certain someone that was meant to get a response from me," Scott said. "I think he deserves a taste of his own medicine." Scott twirled Kim around the floor, positioning them directly in Aaron's line of sight.

"What are you going to do?" Kim remembered Aaron's wandering hands at the wedding. Scott clasped Kim's waist and pulled her closer. He leaned over and whispered in her ear again. "Is he livid yet?" He slid his hand down to rest in the small of her back.

"Stop it! That tickles." Scott dipped her dramatically over his arm with perfect timing. Kim knew that they were being mean, but she couldn't help but laugh at Aaron's fuming face as he approached.

"That's enough, Delaney," Aaron said. "The next dance is mine, I believe."

"Payback is tough, isn't it?" Scott asked with a grin. "You may dance with the young lady, but only if she agrees." Positioned at the edge of the dance area, so their debate wasn't disturbing the other couples. "I did inform her that I expected you two to demonstrate what you learned on my dime at some point this evening, though." Scott turned to seek her permission to hand her over to Aaron. "Kim?"

"Might as well get it over with." Her words were accompanied by a shrug.

"Try to hide your enthusiasm." Aaron tugged her into his arms. They finished the last few measures of the waltz, and then stood in a silent standoff as the band introduced the next number.

"Perfect. A tango," Kim said. "Heavenly humor at work again. At least we won't have to talk to each other."

"Quite the opposite, my dear." As they took their place along with the handful of other couples that were brave enough to attempt the intricate dance, he pulled her closer than necessary. "A captive audience, in relative privacy. I think this is a perfect opportunity to continue our earlier conversation."

Despite his statement, they fell silent as the rhythm of the music brought the familiar moves back. The band's choice of music was a haunting love story made popular in a recent romantic movie. *This is torture,* Kim thought.

"They could have picked a better song." Aaron's words echoed Kim's thoughts.

His voice in her ear brought Kim back to reality. She had been enjoying the feel of his embrace and hoped he couldn't see that tears were threatening. His next words sobered her quickly.

"Why did you leave?" He had resisted asking her this one question directly, knowing her answer would be painful. "What was the real reason? Not the nonsense about finding yourself that you put in your letter." They had adjusted the moves of the tango as their conversation continued. There were several other couples following the more formal moves, so Aaron moved to the edge of the dance area.

"I saw the receipt on your desk," she said. "For the ring."

Aaron's hand tightened on hers and he stumbled briefly on the next movement of the dance. He brought them to a complete stop.

"I couldn't face you, so I left." Kim knew her words sounded breathless. Hopefully he would think it was because of the dance. "Like a coward, I agree, but I had to leave before I ruined whatever thread of friendship we still had." Kim knew she was not being completely honest, but justified the pretense in her mind, knowing that the receipt had solidified her decision. She didn't admit that she had already decided to leave before seeing the incriminating slip of paper.

Kim didn't meet his eyes so she missed his stricken face.

"I can't do this anymore." Kim fled back to the safety of their table. Scott saw her distress and stood as she approached. She walked into his arms. Scott's embrace calmed her down. It had the opposite effect on Aaron.

"We are not done with our conversation." Aaron reached for Kim around Scott.

"You may not be, but I am. I need some air." She grabbed her wrap and headed out to the garden patio. Scott restrained Aaron with a firm hand.

"Sit." Scott quickly took control. Kim reached the refuge of the terrace, she saw Aaron toss his suit jacket over the back of her empty seat. She wasn't the only one feeling that the air in the ballroom had become stifling.

"I'm not finished with her," Aaron said, still preparing to follow her.

"Sit or I will make you sit." Scott's threatening tone was genuine. Aaron wisely complied.

"She finally admitted why she left," Aaron said. He reached across the table and grabbed Kim's untouched glass of tea. "I was right all along. She saw the receipt for the ring. It's over."

"Ring?" Joyce asked.

"Engagement ring." Scott answered his aunt's question, and then turned on Aaron. "I knew she had seen the receipt. I still can't believe you are going to pick Miss Georgiana over Kimberly. You're more of an idiot than I thought you were."

"Gigi? You thought the ring was for Gigi?" Aaron's confusion was evident. He looked frantically from Scott to Joyce. "Kim thought the ring was for Gigi?"

"Oh, my." Joyce's voice cut through Aaron's shock. "That explains so much."

"If the ring wasn't for Gigi...?" Scott's voice trailed off. Aaron's head buried in his hands answered Scott's question. "'Oh my,' is right."

33

Referee or Chaperone?

Scott's laughter did not sit well with the distraught figure next to him.

"I'm so glad you find this funny." Aaron downed the last of Kimberly's drink. He gulped the sweet liquid, but it did nothing to cool his temper.

"You knew she had seen the receipt but had no idea Kim thought the ring was for Gigi." Scott framed his words as a statement, not a question. "That's rich." He shook his head, amazed at the revelation.

"Gigi broke up with me weeks ago. Finally. I'd done all I could to discourage her since before New Year's Eve." Aaron leaned back and rubbed his hand across his face. "How could she ever think I would propose to Gigi?"

"Well, how on earth would she know you'd be planning to propose to anyone else? Obviously, you didn't tell her about breaking up with Gigi, and from what she told me you were widely mercurial for several weeks."

"Mercurial?" Aaron opened one eye. "Please illuminate me with your magnificent eloquence. What shall I do next, pray tell?"

Scott and Joyce laughed, not knowing that Kimberly had been watching from the shadows of the patio. She watched Aaron alternate from stubbornly folded arms to a pitiful pose, elbows on the table, his head buried in his hand. Seeing the laughter at the table, she moved away, seeking solace in the deeper shadows of the dimly lit pathway.

"Between the two of us, I'm certain you have more expertise in the field of Kimberly Calhoun." Scott leaned back with folded arms. "I'll bet my next bonus check on you being able to figure this out."

"Why would she leave if she thought I was going to propose to Gigi? I knew she didn't agree with me dating her, but she could have just told me," Aaron said. "Even the Savannah Rule shouldn't have prevented her stepping in if she thought I was going to marry the girl!"

"The receipt was the last straw, but it's probably not the main reason she left." Scott sipped the coffee that a waitress had just delivered to the table.

"Unless," Joyce started to chime in. Her nephew stopped her with a single glance, knowing she had figured out the mystery.

"We are not going to help him on this part, Aunt

Joyce. He needs to figure it out himself." Scott said, turning back to the man beside him. "Aaron, suffice it to say, she had her reasons."

"I thought she left because she knew my feelings for her had changed." Aaron watched the liquid swirl in the fine crystal coffee mug he held with a tight grip. He finally put the drink down and pushed it away. "You know the real reason she left?""

"Yes." Scott leaned back in his chair. "You might even say it was my fault." As Aaron came out of his seat, Scott knew that he had gone too far.

"Down boy." Scott pushed him back into his chair. "I made a casual observation that she took offense to. You should remember the day well. Lucy's. Lunchtime. Threats were made. Cake was eaten. Do you recall the day?"

"Vividly," Aaron said.

"I promised her that I wouldn't share her secret." Scott ignored the tightly gripped silver-plated knife and offered a friendly pat on Aaron's back. "Since I feel that I'm partly to blame for this misunderstanding, though, I'll offer you a little bit of help."

Aaron opened his eyes, but his arms remained folded. Scott understood that it was going to take more than clearing up the ring misunderstanding to give him any hope. He worded his next statement carefully, not wanting to break his word to Kimberly.

"Go talk to her," Scott said.

"I'm not sure that will do any good at this point,"

Aaron said. "I may have burned all my bridges. Did she tell you that I fired her?" Joyce's nephew came to her rescue as she choked on the sip of coffee she had just taken.

"This just gets better and better." Scott was the only one that seemed to find the situation humorous. He waved off the scowls from the other two and continued. "Convince her to tell you what I told her that day at lunch."

"And if she won't?" Aaron knew there was no hope Kimberly would open up to him at this point.

"If she won't tell you, I will." Scott sighed. "It will mean I have to break my promise to her, but I'm willing to go back on my word if that's what it takes."

"I don't know," Aaron said. Even with his hesitation, he stood and slipped his tuxedo coat back on. "This seems like a lost cause. I'm thinking I'd rather live with the uncertainty than have her complete outright rejection."

"Hope, my friend. I've offered you hope. Take it and run with it," Scott said. "I'll leave my phone on. You may need a referee," he said, then added cryptically, "or a chaperone."

34

On the Terrace

"Kim?" She had heard the patio doors open, so she wasn't surprised to hear Aaron's voice. Silently stepping closer to the stone wall behind her, she hoped he couldn't see her. She was not so fortunate.

"Hiding again?" Aaron asked as his eyes adjusted to the torch-lit terrace. She didn't answer.

"I brought you some coffee." Aaron reached around her and set the fancy glass mug on the ivy-covered wall.

"We need to finish our discussion," he said. Kim could hear the sadness in his voice. It mirrored her own. "Scott and Joyce seem to think we are talking circles around each other. Personally, I think your feelings are unmistakable. You saw the receipt and bolted. Case closed."

She turned, raising her chin defiantly. "Since the case is closed, I guess there's no harm in being brutally honest."

"By all means," Aaron tensed.

"You never told me what the punishment was for breaking the Savannah Rule, but I no longer care. I'm going to break it. How you could possibly think that Georgiana Peterson is the woman to share your life, I don't understand. She doesn't love the Lord like you do, she doesn't like or want children, she flirts outrageously with every handsome man she meets, and she doesn't love you like"—Kim saw Aaron's arched eyebrow and she paused—"like you deserve to be loved."

"Are you done?"

"Almost," she said. "Gigi may not be my favorite person, but I don't wish her ill. I simply couldn't stay and keep my mouth shut. If you love her, then I'm not going to stand in your way." If she hadn't been so intent on keeping the truth hidden, she would have seen his smile. She turned away from him and reached for the still warm mug of coffee.

"Kimberly, Gigi broke up with me. Weeks ago."

Kim's surprise caused her to spill her coffee. Thankfully, it missed her dress and dripped harmlessly down the back of her hand. Aaron handed her his handkerchief and waited patiently as she recovered.

"Weeks ago? When? Why?" Kim's words were barely audible. "You must hate me. I'm so sorry. I knew that I would end up causing problems. I should've left earlier."

Kim took deep breaths, trying to regain her balance. It wasn't a simple task, given her pounding heart. She grappled to fit this new information into the timeline of Aaron's behavior over the past few weeks.

"I ruined everything with Gigi just when you were going to propose and that's unforgiveable. It's your life and I thought I had stayed sufficiently away from your Gigi business."

"Listen to me, Kim." He pulled her back toward him, only holding her hands. "I had been pushing her away since before Christmas, but she didn't seem to be taking the hint. I ignored her at the wedding, pretended to forget lunch dates, and found more than enough reasons to be unavailable. But that wasn't what finally worked."

Kim remained silent.

"It wasn't until after the evening we spent with Mitchell and company that she had finally had enough." Aaron smiled as Kim lifted her eyes finally.

"That's why you were so cranky after the dancing night at the restaurant. You could've just told me she broke up with you. I wouldn't have gloated – at least not to your face." Her comments caused him to smile wider, but knowing she hadn't meant to be funny, he let the remark go without a response.

"Why did she break up with you?"

"She objected to my objections."

"She was mad that you didn't want her flirting with Mitchell? Of course," Kim said as she blinked away tears.

"Not exactly." Aaron ran a finger down the side of Kim's face as he revealed Gigi's real reasons. "She thought I overreacted to *your* attention to Mitchell, not hers."

"That doesn't make any sense. Everyone knows you don't hesitate to intervene if you think I'm having too much fun." She rubbed her arms and shivered as a breeze swept across the terrace. "I still don't understand why you hid it from me."

"I didn't tell you because I knew you'd feel guilty." Aaron slipped off his coat and placed it around her shoulders, knowing her shiver was not just from the coolness of the night air. "All our mutual friends, and family for that matter, have weighed in on our situation. Although they may trust us more than we trust ourselves, I've decided this may be my last chance to ever talk to you, so I need to try to salvage whatever I can."

"That certainly sounds ominous," Kim said with a shaky laugh. "I'm not sure much, if anything, can be salvaged."

"Your assessment is understandable," Aaron said. "I've been a fool."

"I won't disagree." Kim met his gaze boldly.

"Scott seems to think that Gigi is not the real reason you ran away."

"What did he tell you?" She tried to keep the panic from her voice.

"The message is quite cryptic, but he said you would understand." Aaron held her gaze. "Tell me about your discussion at lunch that day at Lucy's." Kim's look turned to disbelief.

"No." She turned away and tightened the coat around her suddenly chilled body. The movement was a poor effort at arming herself against the emotional battle his words evoked.

"He said if you won't tell me, he will." Kim swung around, alarm on her face.

"He wouldn't dare! He promised!" Her anguish overcoming her previous reluctance to speak. Aaron held up his phone. A message from Scott was on the screen.

Kimberly, tell him or I will.

"I don't believe you," Kim said, grasping for a rescue from the dread facing her. "You could have typed that message yourself."

"Shall I call him?" Aaron pulled up Scott's number.

"No." Kim grabbed the phone.

"So, tell me what the big revelation was," Aaron said. "Scott seems to think your secret will be important to me."

Kim shook her head. It was starting to pound, inklings of a headache hinting at the edges. She briefly considered using it as a free pass, but knew it was cowardly. Tempting, but cowardly.

"Fine." She shrugged off his jacket and handed it back to him. "After I tell you, I'm leaving. Do not follow me. At least it will mean this whole fiasco is over." She stared unseeingly across the dimly lit terrace.

"We'll see." Aaron seemed unwilling to concede defeat. He stood right behind her, but didn't reach out to touch her. "I'm waiting."

Without turning back to face him, Kim sighed and summarized the less vulnerable parts of the fateful lunch conversation. Using as few words as possible, she explained Scott's original observations.

"Scott thinks I measure every man in my life against an unattainable ideal."

"Unattainable ideal?" Aaron asked.

"Yes, unattainable. Too high." She could feel the warmth of his body behind her and fought to concentrate on her words. "Actually, 'too specific' were his exact words."

"Kim." Aaron placed a hand next to hers on the brick wall. She flinched and he let his arm drop back to his side. "What did he mean?"

"You, Aaron," she said quietly. "Scott thinks I compare every man in my life to you." She peaked over her shoulder when he didn't respond. "Hilarious, isn't it?" Her hopeless laugh hung in the air.

"That's it?" Aaron finally asked, inching closer to her. "And do you?"

"Do I what?" Kim backed away, lifting the coffee mug as a weapon to keep the distance between them. She sipped what little was left of her now lukewarm coffee, and then slowly set the empty mug on the stone wall.

"I'm calling Scott," Aaron said, his phone once again in his hand. "If you won't tell me the whole truth, I'll have to take him up on his offer."

"Wait." Kim stepped around him, freeing herself from where he had her blocked in against the wall. She wanted to be ready to flee as soon as possible. "Mr. Scott Delaney informs me that in his opinion the evidence points to only one thing." She took a deep breath and decided to get the pain over with quickly. "He says I'm in love with you."

35

Closing Arguments

Aaron's laughter sent her fleeing towards the lobby, planning to ask one of the attendants to retrieve her purse and let Scott know she was leaving.

"Kimberly Nicole Calhoun, come back here. Right now." Aaron's voice cut through the night air, then softened to a plea. "Please." Kim stopped and turned, responding instinctively.

Kim took tentative steps back towards him. As she got close enough, he reached for the ends of her wrap. Kim found herself abruptly pulled against the warmth of his chest.

"I'm so glad you find my distress amusing. Let me go!"

"Never. Stop squirming! Please, Kim." Aaron pinned her arms to her sides. His embrace was gentle and she relaxed. "So, Scott was right. You didn't leave because of the receipt."

She glanced up through lowered lashes to see that he was still amused. Being so close to him made it hard for her to think. Or breathe.

"I had already decided to leave. The receipt just confirmed that my decision was the right one. You were going to propose to Gigi and I wouldn't have been able to keep my opinion to myself. I'm sorry I messed it up for you." Her words tumbled out, confusion and guilt mixing.

"Kimmie." Aaron ran his finger down the side of her upturned face, and tucked a strand of her silky hair behind her ear.

"I know it's crazy, I'm sorry I've ruined our friendship," Kim continued. "I'm sorry Gigi broke up with you after you bought her a ring, I'm sorry to leave you without enough help at work, but I'm going away so you won't have to deal with me anymore." Kim took a shaky breath.

Before she could wind up into another full rant, Aaron stopped her with a kiss. Kim's knees buckled. As she gave into the desires that she had fought against for the last weeks, Aaron's arms tightened around her. He finally set her away from him in an attempt to focus. Her hands remained trapped in his.

"Why did you do that?" She started to pull away, but he refused to release her hands. "To prove you have me at your mercy and that I can't resist you? Fine. You win. Please let me go now, Aaron." Her words were coming in gasps as she finished. Aaron ignored her.

"Tell me, Kimberly." He ignored her question. "Are you?"

"Am I what?" Kim looked at him through a fog of lingering passion and confusion. She closed her eyes and felt Aaron's breath, warm on her neck, as he pressed her for an answer.

"Are you in love with me?"

Before Kim ventured an answer, Aaron's phone beeped. "You've got to be kidding me." He wrapped an arm around Kim's waist, preventing her escape. With his free hand, he pulled out his phone. The call was from inside the ballroom. It was Scott. "I'm a little busy here. This better be really, really important."

Aaron's arm tightened as Kim struggled to free herself. He knew she thought the phone call would distract him into letting his guard down. Instead, he pulled the phone away and pled with her.

"Kim, for the sake of my sanity, please stop wiggling!" Aaron turned back to Scott's call. "What can I do for you Mr. Delaney?" He grinned at her as he listened to Scott's response.

"Chaperone or referee?"

"I was hopeful we were heading towards chaperone," Aaron replied, "until we were rudely interrupted. An additional twenty minutes would be nice."

"I'll give you ten," Scott answered.

"Fifteen and I will forget about your deal to kiss her on request," Aaron said.

"Tough call, but I'll agree," Scott said. "Use your time wisely."

"Kim, you know I won't hurt you, so please stop struggling. It's very distracting." Aaron said as Kim tried to get away once again. He slipped his phone back into his pocket and restated his question. "When did you realize you were in love with me?"

"I admitted no such thing." Kim stilled, and then smiled up at him sweetly. "If you will kindly release me, I'll be on my way."

"I don't plan on ever releasing you."

"Fine," she said. Aaron saw her furrowed brow as she processed his words. Arms folded, she explained as quickly as she could. "You were acting so weird. Pulling away from me one day, all buddy-buddy the next. Then Scott leveled his ridiculous idea."

"Ridiculous?"

"At the time, yes." Her concession didn't satisfy Aaron.

"This is like pulling teeth. Please, Kim, spill it." He grinned and tugged on one of her long curl that had come loose from her fancy clip.

"You're mixing your metaphors, Aaron."

"Scott gave us fifteen minutes. We're rapidly running out of time. Unless you want to have the rest of this conversation in front of an audience, you had better finish your explanation. You realized Scott was right, so why did you leave?"

"Knowing my perspective had changed, and that there

was no way to change it back, I decided I didn't have a choice." Aaron let her move away slightly. "Facing a future with these feelings, I knew I couldn't stay, seeing you every day, being a part of your world, and not love you."

Silence hung between them. Aaron pulled her back into his arms. She started to struggle against him again.

"I'm warning you once again," Aaron said. "Be still." Kim complied so he loosened his hold.

"Could we get this over with? I want dessert." She defiantly wrapped herself in her long scarf.

"Stop being so stubborn and listen to me. I'm so relieved that you're finally talking to me that I'm willing to take my time," he said. "I'm just now beginning to figure this out myself, so be patient."

"Fine." Kim tried to pretend she wasn't wrapped in his arms, on a romantic garden terrace. It didn't work. "Can I go now?"

"Not until you give me your opinion of the ring," he said.

She gasped. "Why would you do that to me? I have no desire to see the ring." Her head was beginning to pound in earnest now.

"Too bad. It's in my jacket pocket. Please retrieve it for me. My hands are a little occupied."

"If I do, will you let me go?"

"Probably not, but I'll agree to consider it," Aaron said. "Your opinion of the ring matters to me, though."

Reaching inside his jacket, she located the small

jewelry box. She blinked away tears, unsure of why he was being so cruel.

"Here." Kim held out the box. Aaron released her. He watched her carefully as she caught sight of the ring. The delicate filigree ring held a small marquis diamond in its antique gold setting.

"How could you?" Kim gasped for breath.

"I see you recognize it," Aaron said.

"That's my ring! It's the one I picked out when Geoff was shopping for Courtney's. How could you do this to me?"

Aaron watched the emotions play across her face. *Patience,* he told himself and slipped the ring back into his pocket.

"Please." Kim took a deep breath and started her pleas again. "I said I was sorry. Just pretend all of it never happened."

"You are delightful." Aaron grinned at her confusion. He saw her frown. "I'm not laughing at you, dear. I'm laughing at the ridiculous situation we find ourselves in."

"What do you mean?" Any path for escape was blocked since Aaron still had her backed against the terrace wall.

"Think, Kimmie. Relax and think." He brushed his lips gently against her cheek. "Of course I knew it was your idea of the perfect engagement ring." Aaron unwrapped the long scarf and unfolded her arms.

"Then why?" Her forsaken sigh made it difficult for Aaron to resist the urge to kiss her again.

"Do you remember the night you were sick?" Aaron asked, pulling her back into his arms. "Do you remember talking about how different your other boyfriends would have handled the ordeal?"

"Ordeal? I'm sorry I was so much trouble."

"Stop interrupting." Aaron placed a finger over her lips. "Pictures of other men taking care of you kept popping into my mind. It was very frustrating." He kissed the furrow between her brows.

"You said something that night that changed my perspective on reality. You may not even remember it." Aaron tilted her chin up, forcing her to look at him. "You said I was your favorite."

She started to protest, just as Courtney had when he first shared the incident with their best friend.

"Wait. Let me finish. Your exact words were that I was your favorite *everything*. That simple statement was life-changing." He paused, hoping his words were finally getting through.

"What are you saying?" Kim's heart was pounding now.

"That night I realized that I had fallen in love with my best friend." He gently wiped the tears that spilled down her cheek. "Sweetheart, the ring is for you."

36

The Verdict

"Me?" Her voice was barely audible and her knees were weak. Aaron's arm around her was the only thing keeping her upright. He traced the lines of her face, sending shivers down her spine.

"What are you doing?" Her voice was noticeably shaky.

"Admiring. Cataloguing, Memorizing," he said. "In case you disappear again. Apparently, you have no idea what torture I've been through over the last two weeks. I practically wore out the scrapbook my mom gave me for graduation."

"I don't understand," she said.

"We should start a support group, my dear. This has been a thoroughly confusing few weeks. Realizing you've fallen in love with someone, thinking that they know you love them, and then they run away because of it, has a tendency to make one a little paranoid."

"You thought I knew you loved me?"

"What do you think I've been trying to say for the last"—he glanced at his watch—"fifteen minutes?" Aaron led Kim to a bench and pulled her around to face him. "You seem to finding this hard to believe. Why?"

"I don't know," Kim shook her head. "You and Courtney adopted me, but I never thought you could see me but anything other than your best friend."

"Kim," Aaron said, cradling her face in one hand. "Do you remember the change that happened when Courtney met Geoff?"

"Yes," she said. "It was pretty funny. Despite all her denials, Courtney couldn't seem to stay away from him." Kim closed her eyes as Aaron ran his thumb across her lower lip.

"For me, it's always been you. From the time you showed up in eighth grade, you were the one that made that difference. We were so young, though, and I'm not as bright as she is," he said. "It's simply taken me this long to realize it."

As Aaron placed soft kisses down her check, neck, and then across her shoulder, Kim lost the ability to speak.

"This silent side of you is intriguing." Aaron's teasing broke through the fog. "Kimberly Nicole Calhoun, I love you. I've loved you for a long time, but was too close to see it. Marry me?"

She stared at him. A soft grin replaced her look of

surprise.

"Kim? Answer me, please." Her fingers inching their way around his neck were distracting him.

"If I say yes, will you kiss me again?"

"Absolutely."

"Then, yes. I'll marry you." Her wish for a kiss was quickly—and thoroughly—granted. He finally forced himself to break the embrace so he could retrieve the ring. He slipped it onto her finger and kissed her again.

"Aaron, I love you," Kim said. "I would've said yes without the kiss, you know."

Scott interrupted Aaron's response. Their chaperone's appearance was unwelcome, but not unexpected. He had given the couple ample time to clear up their misunderstandings.

"They've put out the dessert buffet." Leaning casually against the wall next to Aaron, Scott's trivial statement served as a needed reminder of their lack of privacy. "Not that you guys really care. So, what's up? Anything you need to tell me?"

Kim hugged their friend and thanked him for keeping her secret, knowing now it had put a strain on the friendship between the two men.

"I'm too happy to be mad at you for not telling me the whole truth," Aaron said as they followed Scott back toward the ballroom. "We need to call Courtney and Geoff. They'll be thrilled, if not surprised."

"Courtney will be relieved. I hate that we put her through the agony." Kim said.

"Geoff can check the church calendar for us," Aaron said. "Next week should be good." Kim giggled at his ridiculous statement. He leaned over for another quick kiss as they reached the ballroom doors.

"You're crazy," Scott said. "Annette and Murphy have been engaged for ten months, and their wedding isn't for another six weeks. Good luck getting her to agree to a short engagement, Aaron."

"Six months," Kim said.

"Three weeks," Aaron came back.

"Five months," Kim offered as compromise.

"Four weeks," Aaron said.

"As her lawyer," Scott said, weighing in on the debate. "I must protest that these negotiations do not seem to be equally weighted. Aaron, just surrender now."

"Thank you, counselor." Aaron waved Scott away. "Go on in, we'll be there in two minutes."

"Four months," Kim said, returning to the negotiations. "Final offer."

"If you really loved me, you'd elope with me." With the burden of their estrangement gone, Aaron fell back into the habit of teasing her. Kim's blush told him all he needed to know.

"We both know you're too afraid of Courtney to risk it." She laughed at Aaron's look of stark terror.

"I see how this is going to work," Aaron said. "You are fortunate that I love you beyond all reason. I'm willing to wait for you as long as I must, but you should know that each day I have to wait is one more day of torture."

As they re-entered the ballroom, the band was playing another waltz, so the newly engaged couple took advantage of the romantic tune to celebrate.

"I love you," Kim said. "You *are* my favorite, you know."

"I do know that." Aaron kissed her once more. The applause from their table spread across the ballroom. Aaron laughed as she blushed. He tilted her chin up. "I told you that you deserved someone who would love you, adore you, and protect you. I never thought I would be lucky enough for that person to be me. I love you, Kim."

Epilogue
Will There Be Dancing?

Aaron helped Kim out of their car. He wasn't happy with her.

"I'm going to voice my concerns one last time. I think you should have stayed home." They made their way into the office.

"Go to your meeting. I'm fine. Yesterday the doctor said there were still no signs. It could be two weeks, Daddy dear."

"Or two days. Or two hours." Aaron repeated the doctor's words.

"Joyce is here," Kim said, trying to comfort her nervous husband. "This presentation is an important one. This company represents a big account and Mercer-Chem would be a great fit for their needs. You need to go."

"I know, I know," Aaron said. "I don't have to be happy about it, though." He pulled her into a hug and then gave her a lingering kiss.

"Hey, you two!" Joyce called from the doorway. "You know where that kind of thing will lead!"

Aaron grinned and patted Kim's belly before grabbing his presentation materials.

"I'll be back before lunch. Get whatever tasks done that you think are so important, because then you're going home. Understand?"

"Yes, dear." Kim waved him out the door.

"Don't worry, Aaron," Joyce told him as he left. "We will take care of her."

Over the last few months Kim had cut back on the time she spent in the office, normally coming in only two or three days a week. On the other days she worked at home, handling the accounts for several small family businesses that Chip Larson had sent her way.

Kim settled behind Aaron's desk and started the year-end data entries. An hour later, Joyce confronted Kim. She had been watching the expectant mother closely.

"How far apart are they?"

"I don't know what you mean," Kim lied smoothly.

"Listen, missy," Joyce came around the desk and turned Kim's chair toward her. "I've had two children and I can tell when someone is in labor."

"The first one woke me up." Kim grimaced as she tried to find a comfortable position in Aaron's desk chair. "I knew the presentation for this account was important, though, and I didn't want Aaron to cancel. They're about half an hour apart, but not too painful. I think I was able to hide it from him."

"He's going to be so mad." Joyce reached around Kim and logged off the computer. "We need to go, now."

"I'm fine, really." Kim's protest was interrupted as a contraction hit. She grasped the arms of Aaron's office chair. "Okay, maybe I'm not," she said a minute later.

"Let's go." Joyce helped her up. "Just breathe." They gathered Kim's coat and the overnight bag Aaron had insisted they stash at the office.

"Peggy." Joyce called Kim's assistant into Aaron's office. "Can you please call Aaron and tell him it's time. If he doesn't answer, call Standard's headquarters. That's where his meeting is. They should be able to locate him if the meeting has already started."

The young woman nodded and scrambled for the phone as Kim and Joyce left. Aaron didn't answer. She dialed the corporate office where he was giving his presentation. The receptionist, a newly hired college student, was unhelpful, insisting she couldn't interrupt the meeting for any reason. Peggy was frustrated but recognized the fear in the girl's voice.

Peggy had one more option. She hated taking advantage of her new husband's position, but she was desperate.

"Hello, dear wife." Detective Mitch Harper answered the phone as he stepped out of the precinct office. "I'm just leaving for lunch. Want to join me?"

"Mitch, Kim's in labor and Joyce is taking her to the hospital. Aaron's in a meeting downtown and isn't answering his phone and the receptionist is afraid of losing her job and won't interrupt the meeting."

"Breathe, Peg," Mitch said. "Give me the address and I'll go get him."

"Are you allowed to do that?" Peggy asked. "I don't want to get anyone in trouble."

"It's my lunch break," Mitch reminded her. "They're going to University Hospital, right?"

"Yes, to the new birthing center. Should I keep trying to reach Aaron?"

"No, I'll be there in less than five minutes and seeing a bunch of missed calls will freak him out," Mitch said. "Plus, I want to see Aaron Mercer's face when I break into the meeting flashing my badge. Should be priceless."

Peggy laughed at her husband's antics. "Thanks, Mitch. Call me when you can, okay. Everyone here is anxious."

A few minutes later, Mitchell and the rookie uniformed officer that was shadowing him today entered the lobby of Standard Cleaning. The family-owned company prided itself on being good to its workers, but today a brand-new employee was manning the front desk.

The receptionist knew the meeting down the hall was important but was more afraid of the tall police detective than she was of her new boss. She pointed toward the conference room. Mitch nodded and smiled.

"Stay here," he said to the rookie. "We'll be leaving

quickly."

Mitchell knocked on the door but didn't wait for an answer.

"I'm sorry to interrupt, ladies and gentlemen." He held up his badge as he made his way to Aaron's side. "I'm going to need to borrow Mr. Mercer. His wife is in labor and the doctor says if we don't leave now, he may miss the big event." Peggy had called back in a panic after Joyce had relayed the update from the hospital.

"Go on, son." The company's CEO stood and helped Aaron gather his papers. The man was an old family friend so he was delighted to be of assistance. "I'll call your parents, too, if you don't mind."

Aaron just nodded as he struggled to collect his things and his sanity.

"My car?"

"Will be here when you can come get it," the Vice President of Sales said. "Go!"

Mitchell switched on his emergency lights as they pulled out of the parking lot. The hospital was about twenty blocks away.

"Is that legal?" Aaron asked.

"Do you think it would be safer for me to let you drive yourself to the hospital?" Mitchell asked with a smile. "I'm just protecting the public."

Aaron bolted from the car almost before Mitchell stopped in front of the birthing center. "I'll be back with Peggy after work!" Mitchell called after the soon-to-be new dad.

Kim's soft moan reached his ear as he opened the birthing room door. When she saw him, she burst into tears.

"You're here. I'm so sorry I didn't tell you about the contractions. I thought they would stay far enough apart for you to finish your meeting and then they didn't..."

"Hush, Kimmie. It's okay. I'm here now. I love you." He brushed her hair back from her face and kissed her forehead. "Are you ready for this?"

"I am now," she said. Several hours later, the grandparents had just left. Only Courtney and Geoff Benton remained with the new parents. There had been a steady stream of visitors and at one time the lobby had been full as the crowd of well-wishers waited their turn. The nurses had wisely taken baby Elliot to the nursery during the melee, but had now returned him to his mom.

"I love you, Kimberly Mercer," Aaron whispered to his wife as they watched their best friend hold the newest member of their circle.

"We need to have a big party when you are all recovered," Courtney said. "If the crowd we had here this afternoon is any indication, we'll need to rent a ballroom."

"Will there be dancing?" A drowsy Kim trailed her fingers down the side of Aaron's grinning face.

"Definitely."

~A note from the author~

Thank you for reading Aaron and Kimberly's story. I hope you found encouragement, humor, and a good bit of romance.

I'd love to hear from you. I miss my characters when I finish their stories, so hearing how readers connected with them. is always an encouragement!

You can find me on Facebook (Lyn Ellerbe Books) and my website (Lynellerbebooks.com)

God is the creator of romance. I think He would also say, "You're my favorite."

'...God is in your midst— a mighty Savior! He will delight over you with joy. He will quiet you with His love. He will dance for joy over you with singing.' Zephaniah 3:17 (TLV)

Lyn